Eleanor's Leap

The Journey from Locust Fork, Alabama to the Jumping Frog Jubilee in Calaveras County, California

by Sharon J. Cook

with Lindsey Mullen

Sharon J Cook

Eleanor's Leap

The Journey from Locust Fork, Alabama to the Jumping Frog Jubilee in Calaveras County, California

by Sharon J. Cook

with Lindsey Mullen

Copyright © 2024 by Sharon J. Cook

All rights reserved.

Printed in the United States of America. No part of this book may be used or reproduced in any manner whatsoever without written permission except in the case of brief quotations embodied in critical articles and reviews.

Fifth Estate Publishing, Blountsville, AL 35031

Printed on acid-free paper

Library of Congress Control No:

ISBN: 978-1-958450-10-9

Fifth Estate Publishing

Fifth Estate, 2024

Sharon J Cook

Chapter 1
Locust Fork, Alabama

    The morning sun rose across the serene landscape of Locust Fork, Alabama, waking the sleepy town nestled amid rolling hills, cows, and lush greenery. A gentle breeze whispered through the trees, carrying the sweet scent of magnolias and honeysuckle. The air was filled with the symphony of birdsong, their melodies harmonizing with the soft babble of the nearby Locust Fork River that meandered lazily through the countryside.

    In the heart of this picturesque setting was a quaint house surrounded by a patchwork of wildflowers and tall grasses. Behind this little house, goldfish, turtles, and frogs inhabited a small pond, and in this pond was one very large bullfrog with the very unusual name of Eleanor Roosevelt.

This morning, like so many mornings, Eleanor Roosevelt had woken to the sound of the birds rustling around the pond. Springtime was her favorite season. Each day began with a morning hop-around, checking which flowers had bloomed and which insects had emerged. She stretched her long legs, noted the temperature of the water, checked for any new pawprints in the muddy bank, and did a few laps to get her heart pumping. She knew every nook and cranny of this little pond, but that didn't stop her from exploring. Eleanor Roosevelt was a curious frog. She always wanted to know more.

Satisfied with her inspection, she surveyed the available lily pads. After a few hops, she settled on a small pad in the dappled shade under the honey locust tree. It was a dozy kind of day. She let her eyes close halfway and sleepily watched the dragonflies–settle, unsettle, and settle again–dreaming about what it would be like to have wings that could fly from place to place, landing any moment in a whole new world. Her green flippers were crossed neatly under her chin. Her long back legs dangled in the cool water. The sun was warming her plump little body to perfection. Eleanor Roosevelt was an extraordinary bullfrog having an ordinary day. She couldn't imagine a more peaceful morning.

But—

Up the hill from this haven of peace and solitude, a young woman named Lydia just had her whole world come crashing down around her. After fourteen years and many threats, her husband, Norman, finally left. This time, Lydia somehow knew, for good. As Norman stormed out of the house, he kicked over the potted seedlings Lydia had carefully planted—tender young tomato plants waiting for the last frost to pass so they could be transplanted into the garden.

"You're boring, Lydia," he yelled from the yard.

"You've always been boring, and you always will be, just like this whole county. I'm done with it." He slammed the door of their boring, reliable car and drove off. Lydia watched in muted disbelief though she felt strangely calm.

There was some truth to what Norman said, even if he said it to be mean. Lydia wasn't someone you'd particularly notice. She wore soft, muted colors. She would blend into the background if it weren't for her hazel eyes. Lydia's eyes held a special quality, even as a child. She had eyes that told you she'd really see you, listen, and pay attention. It wasn't just kindness in those eyes–there was something playful, too. Conspiratorial. Creative. On her brighter days, Lydia's eyes were downright magic.

Over the past fourteen years living with Norman, Lydia's eyes had lost some of their sparkle. They were still warm and inviting, but now they held a well of sadness, the twinkle replaced by a dull ache. She remembered the early years with Norman, meeting at a Contra dance, their mutual attraction, and the fun they had cooking together. But she thought now maybe they had married too soon.

She was from this rural county, while he was from a larger city out of the state. They bought this quaint country house together, though Norman said he hoped they could soon move to a bigger city. He longed for more exciting places. But after settling there, Lydia found that she loved it. Other than needing to drive into the city for work, she found herself more and more content in this cottage. Lydia had always been content with a quieter life.

Lydia's upbringing with her grandparents, who were 'flower children' of the '60s, profoundly influenced her musical tastes, values, and worldview. She remembered them spending hours listening to artists, like Bob Dylan, Peter, Paul and Mary, The Rolling Stones, Janis Joplin,

Jimi Hendrix, Elvis Presley, Tab Hunter, and the Everly Brothers.

The reality of Norman's leaving settled on her. Though Lydia didn't love her job, she did it to supplement their income and keep her life in this house with Norman. But Norman was restless. Lydia did most of the chores and tended the garden. Together, they had lived a life of quiet discontent—she, more in love with their home than in love with Norman, and he, disappointed that he had ended up in this small, rural life. It took both of their incomes to pay the mortgage.

She wondered how she would manage. Where would she live if she didn't live here? Lydia was not known to be spontaneous or to jump in without thinking. Most decisions were well-thought-out. But for the first time in a long time, her life felt … unpredictable.

In the wake of Norman's departure, Lydia ran to a wooden bench by the side of the small pond behind her house. Before her, the pond shimmered with the reflections of the surrounding foliage and budding lilies. She plopped onto the weathered seat, not knowing what to do with herself. She dug a hard peppermint from her pocket, a comfort when things felt overwhelming.

The mourning doves cooed overhead. Her gaze wandered across the landscape, seeing but not absorbing the beauty of the flowers in bloom and the play of sunlight on the water's surface, until a large bullfrog sitting on one of the lily pads came into focus.

On impulse, she went for it. She wasn't just trying to sneak up on the frog; she was somehow trying to outpace her own hesitation, to act instead of thinking first, and in that moment, everything changed. This wasn't just an ordinary day anymore; she wasn't her ordinary self. And this wasn't just an ordinary bullfrog.

With both hands, she scooped up the frog, closed her eyes, and pursed her lips. Just as she was about to plant a kiss right on the amphibious lips, she heard a desperate croak. No–not a croak. A human-like voice, a word—

"HEY!"

Lydia opened her eyes and let them refocus on the bullfrog she held inches from her face.

"Hey, stop right there!"

It was unmistakable. This frog could speak, and it was speaking to her.

Chapter 2
No Prince Charming!

Eleanor Roosevelt had just been rudely jerked up off her lily pad, and a pair of coral lips were coming right at her. She was understandably horrified. Her sleepy eyes were now wide open. What happened to her peaceful morning?

Oh, I know, Eleanor quickly surmised, the old Grimms' fairy tale where a frog retrieves a golden ball for a princess in exchange for a kiss, which the frog must have to turn back into a prince. In this story an evil witch had cast a spell turning the Prince into a frog. That old fairy tale had led many women to believe that kissing a frog would bring them a handsome prince, followed by living in a castle and having a beautiful life. *What hogwash!*

"I'm a lady bullfrog. No Prince Charming here!" she croaked.

Surprise clouded Lydia's features as she surveyed the frog clutched in her hands. "Well, then," she sighed. "I'm very disappointed, as I am in dire need of a Prince Charming."

Eleanor rolled her eyes — a movement so unexpected from an amphibian that Lydia raised an eyebrow.

Eleanor's Leap

"Same old story," Eleanor muttered, barely audible. "Some women want a man, a knight in shining armor, to rescue them from their problems and take them to a good life."

"My marriage of fourteen years seems to have ended," Lydia said, her voice barely a whisper. "Norman just left, slamming the door behind him." She glanced at the closed door of the small house behind her, a tremor quivering her lips. "My job won't be enough to keep me in this house for long. It's just a job; I don't love it, and it doesn't pay enough. I'll need a way to increase my income to stay here."

The frog, still in Lydia's grasp, listened intently, drawn to the woman's vulnerability.

"I love living here near the Locust Fork River," Lydia continued, her voice softening as she gazed at the rolling green hills. "The pastures with cows and goats, the redbud trees in spring, the vibrant colors in autumn. I love the quiet, the absence of traffic, a stark contrast to city life. I don't want to leave it."

Lydia turned her gaze to the nearby river just beyond her pond, a gentle smile gracing her lips for the first time. "The river brings so much life: dragonflies, herons, kingfishers, and my favorites—the Louisiana waterthrush with their beautiful songs. I even love the possums and raccoons that steal the birdseed and the frogs that serenade me at night."

This frog, unable to contain herself any longer, let out a low chuckle, startling Lydia.

"I may not be a prince, but I'm not just any talking frog, mind you. I am a rather exceptional bullfrog. I speak English, in addition to Frog Croak, of course. Reading poses no challenge, and I can navigate a roadmap like a seasoned explorer. Internet research? Child's play for this amphibian! And, please, would you put me down?"

Putting the frog down beside the pond, a frown creased Lydia's brow. "A magical frog? So, you are not a prince under a spell, but perhaps you could help me so I don't lose this house."

"Now, Lydia, I don't think you understand what you are capable of, even without magic of any kind. You paint. There are many little pictures you've done right out here. I've seen them. You sing like a bird and strum that guitar. I've heard you. You seem to be unaware of the gifts you have to offer."

Eleanor's Leap

The frog puffed up her chest, a proud glint in her eyes. "But let me introduce myself. I'm Eleanor Ribbitvelt, I mean, Roosevelt. My mother picked me out from all the other tadpoles and gave me this rather unusual name, knowing I was destined to be a remarkable lady frog with remarkable talents. She thought I looked like Eleanor Roosevelt, especially because of my big, beautiful eyes. Ribbit!"

Lydia blinked, taken aback. "Wait a minute," she said, amusement creeping into her voice. "You're telling me you're not just a talking frog, but a talking frog named after the famous former First Lady?"

Eleanor struck a dramatic pose, her nose pointing to the sky. "My dear Lydia, I'm a frog of many mysteries, with a wellspring of abilities some yet to be discovered. But one thing is certain: I am a smart, confident, and undeniably courageous lady bullfrog."

Seeing Lydia's growing amusement, Eleanor regaled her with a background tale. "Now, let me weave you the story of the illustrious Eleanor Roosevelt, the extraordinary woman who hopped her way into the hearts of many."

Eleanor cleared her throat, launching into a lively narration. "Imagine a time when hats were all the rage, and the world was buzzing with change. In 1884, a beacon of grace and resilience emerged—Eleanor Roosevelt. More than just a charming socialite, she was the wife of President Franklin D. Roosevelt and the longest-serving First Lady in American history. She was a trailblazer in her own right."

With each word, Eleanor's voice grew in passion. "She championed civil rights, women's rights, and social justice, leaping into action to make the world a better place. Like a wise old toad, she croaked for equality and justice with every hop."

Eleanor paused and considered the sad woman squatting on the bank before her: "Now, tell me about yourself."

"Well, I'm Lydia. I live in this house up close to the pond. This has been an awful day. Norman thinks he will do better without me. He is tired of living a conventional life. He wants a new life. He didn't like doing chores around our house. He left with our car and his guitar. I am alone now. I'm sad and angry."

"I am sorry you are sad and angry. That is not the way you prefer to be. I know a great deal about you, Lydia, perhaps because you live near my pond. Knowing about people close to me is another unique magical ability, along with talking in English and searching Google. How I do any of these, I am not certain. I've been roaming the Web since I was a tadpole, but you are the first human I have encountered."

An outrageous idea tickled Lydia, changing her mood and hanging like a balloon of hope. She looked down at Eleanor's long, powerful legs. A mischievous glint came into her eyes. "Speaking of remarkable talents," she began, a hint of a smile playing on her lips, "Are you very good at jumping, Eleanor?"

Chapter 3
More Beyond

"Lydia," Eleanor croaked, her voice filled with enthusiasm, "I'm quite the athlete. Jumping has been my passion since I left life as a tadpole. I can leap higher and farther than any frog in this pond! My exceptional jumping skills have served me well in catching my meals, leaving all the other bullfrogs in the shallows," she continued, her voice rising with each word. "I've always considered myself the undisputed champion jumper in these parts."

Eleanor's voice dropped to a conspiratorial whisper, "Actually, I've harbored a secret ambition for as long as I can remember—to compete in the legendary, celebrated frog-jumping contest in Calaveras County. It is the equivalent to the Olympics for frog jumping."

Lydia, astounded, "You have heard of this contest made famous by a short story of Mark Twain? 'The Celebrated Jumping Frog Contest of Calaveras County?' I read it in high school."

"Of course!" Eleanor said. "It was published in 1865 and started Twain's career. Back then, still known as Samuel Clemens, he had gone out west during the gold rush days to escape the Civil War and try to make some money himself. Back in the mid-1800s, during the height of the Gold Rush, there wasn't much for the 49ers to do when they weren't prospecting for gold or silver. So, some of the rowdier men would get drunk and find anything and everything to bet on. One of the things that they sometimes bet on was who could capture a frog that would jump farther than anyone else's frog."

"Yes!" Lydia said, wondering how could this bullfrog, born in her little pond, know about this story? "Eleanor Roosevelt, how do you know about that story?"

Eleanor continued, "As I said, I am an expert at roaming the World Wide Web. And I'm a very curious frog and want to learn about so many things. I am, of course, most interested in anything about frogs, and this story is about a frog-jumping contest.

"And, not just that, I long to see more than what's happening in this pond. I've also learned the world is so much more than what is here in this little pond in Locust Fork, Alabama. I'd love to venture beyond. You see, and there is another story:

"Earlier this spring, a blue-black raven flew by and dropped me a gift, a silver spoon. Made of gleaming silver, it is slender and elegant, fitting perfectly within my tiny grip. Etched into the silver surface are the words: *'There is More Beyond.'* More beyond what? I wondered. What did it mean? This little spoon has fired my curiosity and desire for adventure, to see what exists in places beyond this little pond."

Lydia's smile widened. Not only was this frog capable of magic. Not only did she carry the inspirational name of Eleanor Roosevelt. She was also a potential champion–an amphibian with grand aspirations!

Eleanor's Leap

Lydia also knew that these days, there was the potential of a very big purse for the person bringing the winning frog to the contest in Calaveras County. And, as to the message of the spoon? Perhaps she and Eleanor were meant to discover what's *'more beyond'* together. The idea of competing in the frog jumping contest, fueled by both their desires – Lydia's need for money to keep her home and Eleanor's thirst for a bit of adventure – was suddenly an undeniable possibility.

"Well, Eleanor Roosevelt," Lydia said, her voice brimming with newfound excitement, "it seems we have a shared goal. Perhaps a trip to California is exactly what we both need. And I am beginning to see that what I need is a whole new perspective on my life. I seem to have lost that fire of energy and confidence that used to fuel me."

Chapter 4
Meeting Buttercup

"Lydia, you can do the driving, right?" said Eleanor. "I may have some magical skills, but cross-country driving is not one of them. That will be your job. But, if Norman took the car, what would we drive?"

"There was a time, earlier in my relationship with this husband, when we went to art and music festivals in an old Volkswagen Beetle. I still have her. She's a 2004 VW beetle, a bit of a fixer-upper. I recently got all the rust knocked out, gave her a fresh coat of yellow paint, and named her 'Buttercup.' Like us, I think she's ready for a new adventure."

Eleanor hopped over to Buttercup's place in the garage. Looking both intrigued and amused she said, "Ah, Buttercup! A classic beauty, I see. I like the name. It suits her well."

"Now, I must warn you," Lydia said, "Buttercup has her quirks. She isn't the speediest vehicle on the road. She runs pretty well, except on the days she decides not to cooperate. We'll fix her up whenever she fancies a breakdown."

Eleanor chuckled. "Buttercup, you're a diva, aren't you? Don't worry, we'll take good care of you. I'm sure we'll have some interesting stories to tell about your peculiarities by the end of this trip."

Eleanor gave a little hop of excitement. "My job is planning the route and navigating. I've checked the maps and consulted Google, and it's an easy twelve-day drive to Calaveras County and the Frog-Jumping Festival. Here's a list of the places we'll be driving through: Memphis, Tennessee; Little Rock, Arkansas; Oklahoma City; Amarillo, Texas; Albuquerque, New Mexico; Flagstaff, Arizona; Las Vegas, Nevada; Yosemite National Park; and finally, Angel Camp, California. This route will also allow us to see many places across the U.S. along the way."

"Now that you have the route mapped out," Lydia said, "I can pack Buttercup. We'll camp along the way. I can't afford to stay in a hotel. I have this old army pup tent that belonged to my husband. It will have to do. I'll bring my air mattress to make it more comfortable, though since I can't stand up in this old tent, it will never be comfortable."

"Camping out, roughing it a bit, will make it feel like a true adventure," Eleanor croaked happily.

Lydia smiled. "Eleanor Roosevelt, my talented froggy friend, the next issue is figuring out how to pay for some additional travel expenses. I've got some savings to kickstart our adventure, but we'll need more money along the way. I don't know how that will happen, but we can't let that stop us. I'm counting on your winning jump in the frog jumping contest in Calaveras County to get us the big bucks."

Eleanor puffed out her chest with pride. "I hate to brag, Lydia, but you can count on me! I'll give it my best leap, and we'll make a splash at that contest!" After a moment, Eleanor added, "And you, Lydia, can supplement our funds along the way with singing and selling your paintings."

Lydia's brows rose in surprise. "I've never really considered that anyone would want to buy those paintings, and I've not considered myself a singer people would pay to hear. Friends do say I sing like Mary Travers of Peter, Paul, and Mary."

"Lydia, I've heard you play and sing. You are like one of the birds that frequent our pond. And your paintings are lovely. Are you aware of how many times you added my portrait somewhere in your pieces?"

Lydia giggled. "I guess not! I'm flattered that you noticed, but the money that will make a difference will be you winning that contest, so I guess we need to do a little practicing for you to have the best chance of jumping the furthest. Then, I think we're ready to go."

Eleanor gave another short hop. "Absolutely, Lydia! And the fact that we can work and practice jumping while on the road makes it all the more special. It's like turning a road trip into a grand adventure with a purpose."

"Ellie, as requested, I put together a wood box with slats on the side. We'll put it on the front seat, high enough for you to sit on and see out the windshield. There's a pan of water in the box so you can keep moist. If we bring my stack of completed paintings and my painting supplies, we'll need to tie most of the camping gear on top of Buttercup. She's not very roomy."

Lydia shook her head in disbelief. "I feel like I'm finally on my own path and being pushed off a cliff at the same time. And, traveling with a frog as a companion, a magical frog to boot? Definitely new! But here we are, talking about 'we' and 'us,' ready to face the unknown. Life has a funny way of surprising us, doesn't it, Eleanor?"

"*There is more beyond.*" Eleanor smiled to herself.

"Buttercup is gassed up and ready to go," Lydia said. "Let's do this!"

Chapter 5
On to Memphis

With Buttercup packed, the house locked up, and Eleanor Roosevelt perched on her wooden box on the front passenger seat, Lydia left her Locust Fork home.

It was a lovely April morning, and the Alabama countryside unfolded its rolling hills, quaint farmhouses among oak trees, green pastures of grazing cattle and goats, and the occasional horse farm. Yellow and purple wildflowers dotted the roadside.

Though she always kept her hands on the steering wheel, Lydia's eyes wandered the landscape as she drove. She loved the blooming redbud trees and the draping wisteria. She loved the way the light played on the clouds and the rain pouring down somewhere far across the horizon. She loved the red-shouldered hawk perched on the telephone wire. She loved this place, and she loved this new feeling of freedom that was washing over her.

Lydia was happy to have Eleanor navigate. She'd always struggled to keep her mind on directions and was prone to getting lost, even in places where she'd lived for years. Eleanor beamed confidently, croaking, 'turn right here' and 'turn left there' as she consulted the map. She was patient when Lydia missed a turn, quickly and calmly righting their route. Soon, they passed a sign welcoming them into Tennessee. Buttercup rumbled along contentedly.

At some point, Lydia realized the cars before her were slowing down. She snapped her attention from the landscape, looking for an explanation for the slowdown on the highway–maybe construction or a tractor headed down the road. She was surprised to see that they weren't even on the highway anymore. They were in a line of cars queuing up to enter some kind of estate. She looked around for some explanation and saw a large blue sign with swooping cursive writing, "Graceland: Home of Elvis A. Presley."

She looked sympathetically over at Ellie. "Everyone makes a wrong turn sometimes. Don't worry. I'll look for a place to turn around, and we'll get back on track." Eleanor looked back slyly. She was keeping them on course to Calaveras County, of course, but she was a frog with a bigger agenda.

"Well, Lydia, it's not so much a wrong turn as a small side adventure. I thought we'd make a little side trip to pay respects to Elvis. I know you like his music.

Then we can camp alongside the Arkansas River west of Memphis tonight."

Lydia grinned. "You are sneaky, Eleanor! Elvis may have been before my time, but I still know all about him. My grandparents had his records. As a kid, I couldn't get enough of his music."

Eleanor croaked back with excitement, "He was way before my time, too, but I learned to wiggle, swim, and groove by copying his hips and listening to his music. Everything is on the Web!"

Together Lydia and Eleanor belted out Elvis Presley's "Jailhouse Rock" together:

> *The warden threw a party in the county jail.*
> *The prison band was there, and they began to wail.*
> *The band was jumpin', and the joint began to swing.*
> *You should've heard those knocked-out jailbirds sing!*
> *Let's rock. Everybody, let's rock.*
> *Everybody in the whole cell block was dancin'*
> *to the Jailhouse Rock!*
> (Written by Jerry Leiber and Mike Stoller, Performed by Elvis Presley, 1957)

Lydia giggled as Eleanor shimmied to the song. But her smile faded with a stab of disappointment. "But, Ellie, no matter how much we love Elvis, a ticket into the Graceland mansion is expensive. I don't have the money for that. We just have to keep driving."

Ever confident, Eleanor was not deterred. "How about this? I've looked up Graceland on the Web. We can see the graves of Elvis and his parents and the meditation garden for free. Maybe that's enough. I just need to pay my respects. Plus, there's a pond in this meditation garden. I will always vote to go to a pond!

Anyway, Lydia, we're already here."

Lydia's grin returned despite herself. "Alright, Eleanor. You win. Let's go see the King."

Chapter 6
A Side Trip to Graceland

A crowd of tourists was gathered at the mansion's gates, waiting to get inside to pay their respects. Lydia slipped Eleanor into her backpack, deciding that a magical bullfrog might be a little much to introduce to this crowd. The brick wall surrounding the gates was almost entirely covered with the signed names of Graceland visitors. Lydia found a little corner, pulled out a Sharpie, and wrote: *Lydia Watson and Eleanor Roosevelt, an Extraordinary Bullfrog. We love you, Elvis.*

Lydia and Eleanor entered Graceland with Ellie tucked away in Lydia's backpack. As they approached the meditation pond, Lydia knelt and opened the bag so Eleanor could look around before hopping onto the ground beside Lydia.

Eleanor took in the sight of the garden. She'd seen this place in pictures, but it was different in person. The meditation pond was smaller than she'd imagined. The artificial flowers made it colorful, if a bit garish. Well, Ellie thought, it's hard to deny that the King was himself a bit garish, so I guess that fits.

Many large, granite gravestones surround the meditation pond, marking the family graves: Elvis, of course, and his parents, his grandfather, his great-grandmother, his great-great-grandmother, his twin brother Jessie, who died at birth, his daughter, Lisa

Presley, and her son. Lydia and Eleanor both felt a wave of reverent sadness. Such vibrant people now lay still in this quiet garden.

Eleanor felt her energy shift as she looked around the garden. Elvis Presley wasn't about reverent sadness. He was about life! And sensation! And moving your hips! She shook off her reverie and took a big leap, heading straight for the pond. The cool green water was just what she needed to feel alive again.

Just as Lydia realized Ellie was no longer beside her, she heard a big splash in the no-longer tranquil pond. Eleanor had made it to the water, but she wasn't the only one looking to shake things up in this garden. A little boy with a Braves cap atop a mass of curly red hair was close behind, hands outstretched to catch the slippery bullfrog.

He dove straight into the pond with a loud splash. A woman with matching red curls — she had to be his mother — leaned in to try to grab her little boy and promptly fell in herself. Any shred of dignity the mother was trying to hold onto was lost as she attempted to exit the pond and slipped, causing another disruptive splash to spray the formerly somber graveside viewers.

Lydia's hand covered her mouth as she watched a man attempt to rescue the mother, only to become another casualty of the slippery rocks. The whole family was laughing now as they squished through the pond's muck. Any sense of reverence in the garden was gone. People around were clapping and laughing along. It was quite a scene when security guards showed up to try to restore some order.

As the parents finally extricated themselves from the water, Lydia's eyes landed on the little boy, who was now eyeing the gravestones with keen focus. She followed his gaze to see Eleanor Roosevelt, with puckered lips, planting a solid kiss on the gravestone of the King.

Eleanor's Leap

"Huh!" Lydia huffed indignantly. "And she wouldn't kiss me!"

After the pond debacle, Eleanor and Lydia made a quick exit from Graceland. One security guard watched with a little too much interest as Eleanor hopped down the garden path, but what was he going to do, arrest a frog?

Once they made it to Buttercup and were on the road, they found a place to camp west of Memphis.

The next morning, they would head to Breckling Riverfront Park in Little Rock, Arkansas.

Chapter 7
Breckling Riverfront Park
Little Rock, Arkansas

"I learned from the internet," Eleanor said, "that this Breckling Riverfront Park is one of the country's best public parks of this sort and right in the heart of Little Rock along the Arkansas River. It's a nice place to stretch our legs. My long frog legs need stretching. The online reviews tell us there is art in the park and lots of interesting things to do. Lydia, you could set up a booth and sell some of your paintings here. It's a perfect day and a perfect place. Pull them out and set up your station."

"I don't know." Lydia looked through her paintings, wondering again if anyone would be interested in her little paintings of flowers, trees, a pond, and, yes…frogs. "What if no one looks or if they look then walk away?"

"So what if they walk away? Nothing lost. You have to try, and they really are lovely. I think they would brighten up many rooms."

"Okay, I guess there's nothing to lose in trying. But first, I'll wander about and look at all there is to see here."

"I have something I want to do while you wander," Eleanor said.

Lydia headed off to the sculpture garden and many unique displays in the park. A few hours later, she found a spot to display some of her art. An idea hit her. She brought out her guitar and sang Mary Travers' folks songs from the '60s to see if it would draw people in.

> "If I had a hammer, I'd hammer in the morning,
> I'd hammer in the evening, all over this land.
> I'd hammer out danger, I'd hammer out a warning.
> I'd hammer out love between my brothers and my sisters
> ah-aaah….All over this land….."
> (Written by Pete Seeger and Lee Hays as "*The Hammer Song*" 1949, Performed by Peter, Paul and Mary, 1963)

As for Eleanor, after her morning stretches and a lively hop about the park, she headed to the nature center. She chuckled to herself as she considered the idea of a 'nature' center. What funny ideas humans had. Here they have this beautiful river surrounded by meadows and forests and filled to the brim with plants and insects and animals. It was all waiting for them. All they had to do was learn to see it.

But what did they do? They took individual creatures, separated them from their whole environment, imprisoned them in a scene they re-created, and called it a 'Nature Center.' Eleanor Roosevelt sighed. It was like shooting a bird out of the sky to try to understand flight. Humans were ridiculous sometimes. There was no other explanation.

As she faced the entrance to the Nature Center, Eleanor steeled herself for what she would see when she went inside. She'd read about the Center and places like it but had never seen one before. She puffed up her chest with righteous indignation. She hadn't mentioned it to Lydia, but she had a greater purpose for this part of their adventure. She was going to find her captive relatives, and she was going to set them free.

The air in the Nature Center was filled with the sounds of croaking frogs and was moist with the humidity of their artificial habitats. As she moved toward the sounds of life, she took in the displays around her. A part of her couldn't help but admire the carefully written placards, each describing characteristics and habitats with precise attention. Eleanor was a researcher herself; she could sense the enthusiasm of the naturalists who'd written these descriptions.

But she shuddered as she looked above the text. She knew there would be captive frogs here, but she hadn't realized there would also be dried frog bodies on display, pinned in poses under glass cases. Eleanor paused for a moment. No rescuing these relatives. She kept moving toward the echoing frog songs down the hall, finally arriving at the terrariums filled with living creatures.

She felt her heart dip as she gazed at the rows of displays. These frogs were prisoners. Sure, they were well fed, and their glass cages were clean, but they didn't know the joy of a pond or the thrill of a river. They didn't get to find their mates or find their food. They didn't get to watch the raindrops ripple the water or see the tadpoles find their legs. They weren't free.

Eleanor approached the first terrarium. She peered up at the frogs inside. They looked back, taking in her webbed feet and magnificent shimmering green skin with curiosity and resignation. Emboldened by the sight of her soon-to-be-rescued captives, Eleanor took in a deep breath and then began to croak a magical melody, hoping to communicate her intentions to the captive frogs. "My fellow amphibians! You deserve a life beyond the confines of glass walls. I am here to set you free."

Eleanor's Leap

Her enchanted song echoed through the Nature Center, and the other frogs responded with a chorus of croaks.

As she hopped closer to the first terrarium, she said, "Amphibious Comrades! I come with a vision of freedom and adventure, of a life beyond these glass walls. The Arkansas River awaits you, where you can live as nature intended. In tune with the gift of my raven friend, there is more to life beyond the confines of these walls."

Eleanor Roosevelt was on a noble mission, but she couldn't resist the opportunity to add a little drama to the task. She was, among many other things, a performer. She gestured to an invisible audience as she approached the next terrarium.

"So, who do we have here?"

She glanced at the placard beneath the glass. "Here, we have Sam. Sam is a common green frog, *Lithobates clamitans*, a bronze frog with dark mottling on his head, chest, and under his legs. He has a yellow lip and throat.

He's not quite as large as a bullfrog like me. But he is unique in having six different kinds of croaks. Sometimes, he sounds like a guitar. Hmm. He could sing with Lydia."

Sam belched, "Croak...Croak?"

Eleanor continued her stroll, pausing again at the next enclosure.

"And, here, we have Sylvester. *Anaxyrus American*, an American Toad." What was he doing here? "Sylvester, you're not a frog! Toads don't measure up. You have short hind legs and can't really jump, so you crawl. Also, you just aren't pretty. Toads have dry, warty skin."

Eleanor touched her shoulder with her webbed hand, grateful for her slick and shiny skin.

Sylvester glared back at her. "Croak...Creek...Croak. You are pretty insulting, Eleanor Roosevelt!"

Eleanor sighed. "Lydia would say I'm not being friendly. But I say I'm discriminating. The Cambridge dictionary says that means I have good taste, I know quality and what is best." She hesitated. "But discrimination can also describe being prejudiced against other creatures, judging them as inferior. I see that is mean; they are creatures just like me, just different. The first Eleanor Roosevelt, the President's First Lady, wouldn't want me to talk like this. So, okay, Sylvester, I apologize. I'll include you in our plan."

Before Sylvester could open his mouth to respond, Eleanor launched into her next introduction.

"Here is Barbara, a barking Tree Frog, *Hyla gratiosa*. She's small, just 3 inches, and bright green with dark brown spots. She can change her colors quickly. Her croak is very loud, kind of like a barking dog. Barbara's close relatives are found high in treetops. I bet living in this terrarium is not good for you!"

Barbara: "Arf...Arf!!"

Eleanor smiled with affection. She looked up and

down the nature center hallway and saw how many frogs were being held there, not to mention all the other creatures. Her gaze landed on one large terrarium in particular. She had a lot of rescuing ahead of her, but first, she had one more introduction to make. She hopped over.

"Here we have a classic crowd favorite, the great American bullfrog, *Lithobates catesbeianus*. Meet Harriet! Like me, Harriet is among the largest frogs in North America. We can be found in freshwater ponds, lakes, and marshes. We can grow to eight inches long and weigh up to a pound and a half. Our croaks are kind of like a cow mooing. We're among the largest frogs in North America."

Harriet responded politely. "Well, good morning, Eleanor Roosevelt. I've heard about you. Quite an amazing magical frog you are! Welcome to our home in the Nature Center at Breckling Riverfront Park. How do you like my aquarium? It is like a condo with everything I need."

Eleanor nodded in response, barely taking in what Harriet was saying. She puffed up her chest, her webbed feet tapping the floor with determination. Raising her voice so that all the frogs and toads could hear, she said imperiously, "I am Eleanor Roosevelt, an American bullfrog with some rather unique abilities. I have come to rescue you poor amphibians from this nature center, to get you out of these fancy terrariums and lead you to the Arkansas River.

"Think of me like Moses leading the Jewish people out of Egypt to the promised land. There's a world out there beyond these walls—a world of ponds, rivers, lily pads, worms, and dragonflies. We were not meant to be confined like this. I want to lead you to a life of adventure, where every leap is a step towards freedom, all kinds of critters there for you to eat, and—"

Before Eleanor could finish her proclamation, Harriet

interrupted skeptically. "And, Eleanor Roosevelt, what about the herons, kingfishers, and really big fish? Aren't they out there in the Arkansas River, too? And don't they also like to eat?"

Eleanor was caught off guard, but she recovered quickly. "Yes, of course. But there are lots of hiding places. You just have to stay alert."

Harriet scoffed. "You realize here in the Nature Center; we don't have to hunt for our supper. It's brought right to us—crickets...worms...flies...all the very best. We have water and warmth here. So why should we leave?"

Eleanor rose to the challenge with a wise gleam in her eyes. She responded to Harriet, but her voice was directed at all the creatures in the center. "Yes, there may be challenges, but isn't that what makes life worth living?"

Eleanor's passion came through in her speech. *This was important!*

"We creatures need adventure to feed our curiosity, to dive into new waters, to learn and grow. Staying here may be safe, but it's a stagnant life. We are resilient creatures. I'm sure you will be able to face whatever comes your way. Trust me, the Arkansas River will be a haven, a paradise!"

Silence.

"Don't you want freedom? Everyone wants freedom! Go where you want to go. Choose your own trees, ponds, lily pads, and find your own food. Do what you want to do. Be independent?"

Harriet was shaking her head, her front legs stubbornly on her hips. "Eleanor, you are not so smart. Do you know that out there in the natural world, we frogs and toads don't often survive more than a few years? Here, with the caretakers, it's possible to live for decades!"

Eleanor hadn't anticipated this. Could it be that these

Eleanor's Leap

frogs really didn't want to live under the bright blue sky? That they didn't long for the freedom of swimming through the pond's depths or floating down the creek on a summer day? Could it be that this life in these small terrariums was enough for them? Eleanor couldn't believe it.

"Frogs, listen to me! Where is the joy of decades in a boring, predictable life? Frogs, you have to hear me. There is more beyond!"

The frogs exchanged skeptical glances and uneasy croaks, unsure of this charismatic, magical frog's ideas. The debate between Eleanor Roosevelt and the captive frogs echoed through the nature center, a great debate of freedom and risk versus captivity and comfort unfolding in the heart of Little Rock, Arkansas.

After a while, Harriet stopped the debate by calling for a vote. "All who vote to follow this frog out into the Arkansas River—croak now!"

Eleanor puffed up her chest and looked around the hall. She looked at Sam and then Sylvester. Both looked at their feet, not making a sound. Even tiny Barbara ducked her head to avoid looking Eleanor in the eyes. All that could be heard now was the whirring sound of the water pumps circulating filtered water through each enclosure.

Eleanor was stunned.

"That settles it," Harriet said decisively. "We appreciate your enthusiasm, but we've grown accustomed to this life. It's safe and predictable, and we have food delivered regularly. Why would we leave all this behind? We've decided. We'll stay here. Thanks for visiting! I'm going back to sleep."

Deflated, Eleanor Roosevelt hopped out of the Nature Center, aimlessly wandering the park's paths. Her great escape plan hadn't gone at all as planned.

Meanwhile, across the park, Lydia's day had also gone differently than expected. After Eleanor's encouraging words, she'd set up her watercolor paintings and laid out her open guitar case while she played her favorite songs. Like Eleanor said, what did she have to lose?

To her surprise, people not only smiled as they passed by, but many dropped dollar bills and loose change into her guitar case. People asked her about her watercolor paintings between songs, commenting on the vibrant colors and serene scenes. Lydia shared stories about her lovely pond in Locust Fork, beaming with pride for the place she called home. One by one, the paintings disappeared, finding new homes with people who appreciated the beauty of the natural world and the way that Lydia had captured it in her art.

Lydia shook her head in disbelief as she packed up her guitar and muttered to herself. "Maybe I am a real artist, after all. I can't wait to tell Eleanor that she was right. Where is that extraordinary bullfrog anyway? It's almost time to go."

Lydia looked across beautiful Breckling Riverfront Park, grateful for the warm reception she'd found here. A wide smile crossed her face as she took in the sight of the river and the trees all bathed in golden light. The sun would be setting soon. She opened her mouth and sang out modified lyrics to John Denver's "Leaving on a Jet Plane" across the park, hoping Eleanor would hear her and get the message.

> *All my bags are packed. I'm ready to go.*
> *I'm standing here beside ol' Buttercup ...*
> *I'd hate to say goodbye and leave without you.*
> *So please come round and find ol' Buttercup...*
> *I'm leaving on a jet plane...*
> *Don't know when I'll be back again.*
> (*"Leaving on a Jet Plane"* by John Denver, 1966)

Eleanor was still moping along, grumbling to herself about freedom and courage, when she caught the sound of Lydia's song. "What's that I hear? Lydia singing!" (Hop...hop...hop). Her mood lifted immediately when she saw Lydia's face. She didn't even have to ask how the day went. She could tell by Lydia's posture that it had gone well. For a moment, Eleanor forgot about the Nature Center and the self-satisfied frogs. She was happy for her friend.

Lydia caught Eleanor up on her day, recounting the people who bought her paintings and listened to her songs. She was glowing with a new confidence and relieved that they had a little more cash for the adventure ahead. Once they had Buttercup packed up and were on the road again, Lydia took a breath and glanced at Eleanor. "Enough about my day. What about you? Did you find anything interesting in the Arkansas River? Make any new friends?"

"Well," Eleanor started, "not exactly...." She launched into the story of the Nature Center, giving Lydia all the details about the dried frogs and the terrariums, her disturbance reemerging as she recounted Harriet's speech and the silence of the frogs when the vote was called.

"I just don't understand that there are creatures who choose a safe, predictable life over freedom. Where is the growth in that? Where is the challenge? The adventure? Curiosity? These other amphibians don't think like me."

Lydia could hear the hurt in Eleanor's voice. She knew that this rejection was very personal for her friend. She was gentle in her response. "Ellie, I think you were brave to try to rescue those frogs, but I guess I can also see where they are coming from."

Eleanor did a double take—Lydia, too? Didn't anyone else long for an adventure?

Almost as if she could hear Ellie's thoughts, Lydia said, "You know, Norman always really longed for a more adventurous life. He was always talking about it. And, it sort of scared me."

Eleanor hadn't expected this. Norman was supposed to be the villain here. Eleanor was a rescuer!

"I know that by the time he left, things had gotten pretty bad, and I'm not saying he was right about the way he treated me. But, Ellie, sometimes people—and frogs, I guess—can't walk out an open door into adventure. Freedom is scary, and I must admit that I was scared when Norman talked like that. I was numb. My life was just comfortable enough, like the frogs at the Nature Center said. And it was predictable and familiar. The day that Norman left was the day adventure just snuck up and found me in spite of myself...in the form of an American bullfrog—you!

"And if I hadn't found you, who knows where I would be right now? I definitely wouldn't be driving Buttercup down this highway. And I wouldn't have played my music for strangers or put my art up for sale." Lydia blinked back tears as she thought about how far she had come in just a few short days. She was proud of herself, and she was grateful.

"I guess I needed a rescuer that day, but it wasn't Moses or Prince Charming who showed up. It wasn't a hero in a cape or even a prince with a castle. It was a friend, Ellie—a friend pushing me toward going *beyond*. You rescued me by being my friend."

Eleanor Roosevelt felt tears welling up. She had wanted those frogs to feel the joy of liberation, but she hadn't considered what it would take for them to feel safe enough to hop out into the world.

"You're right, Lydia. You're really right. I guess those frogs just weren't miserable enough. They were complacent with the life they had. Change was forced on you by Norman leaving, whether you wanted it or not. Complacency was no longer an option."

Chapter 8
Rain & The Old Army Tent

After a couple of hours of driving into the night, they stopped on the shore of Lake Stanley Draper near Oklahoma City. Lydia quickly set up camp. A storm was coming. Lydia was zipping up the door on the old army pup tent as the rain began to fall—first just a couple of drops and then a full-on downpour hammering down on the thin canvas.

"Ugh, this old thing leaks worse than a sieve," she muttered as she gathered her small pile of belongings. Dampness was seeping up from the floor, and the storm pounded out an unwelcome lullaby. How would she get any sleep tonight?

"Hey, at least it keeps the wind out, right?" chimed a cheerful voice from outside the tent. Ellie bounced in, a puddle of water trailing behind her.

Lydia winced. Ellie seemed to revel in the downpour. She hopped back out, the rain cascading down her face.

Lydia sat alone in the old army pup tent, her fingers tracing the faded olive drab fabric as raindrops danced a mournful ballet on the canvas. It was a tent that had seen better days, and the relentless rainstorm outside revealed its age and wear. Leaks sprang from various corners, and puddles formed around her, slowly encroaching on the small, dry space she had left.

The tent was Norman's, a relic from his military days.

The steady patter on the tent's roof was a relentless reminder of her current predicament.

Tears welled up in her eyes, blurring the already rain-streaked canvas. Lydia's mind drifted back. Memories of her wedding day, filled with hope and promise, surfaced. Then came the arguments, the silences, the slow unraveling of their dreams. A choked sob escaped her lips.

"Hey, are you okay in there?" Ellie's voice, muffled by the rain, cut through Lydia's thoughts.

"Yeah, I'm fine," Lydia mumbled, wiping her tears with a damp sleeve. But she wasn't fine. She felt like a drowning woman, lost in a storm with no end in sight.

The joy that she had felt earlier in the day seemed silly now. So, she had sold a few paintings in a park — what difference did that make? Her marriage was over; she might lose her home. She didn't know who she really was or what she even wanted. She was traveling with a frog as a companion, for goodness' sake. What was she doing with her life?

As the night wore on, the rain continued its relentless assault. The leaks in the tent multiplied, and the chill seeped into Lydia's bones. Would she ever find shelter from this storm?

But then it was morning. The first rays of dawn peeked through the clouds, chasing away the rain. Exhausted, but relieved that the rain had finally stopped, Lydia emerged from the damp tent. The sun was coming out. The hard night was over at last.

"Well, that thing definitely needs to be retired," Eleanor declared, surveying the puddle-soaked canvas. "Don't worry, Lydia. We'll get you a new tent in Oklahoma City. And you know what? You can even get one tall enough to stand up in!"

Lydia forced a smile. Buying a new tent was doable. Building a new life? That was a whole different story.

Eleanor's Leap

Chapter 9
Kanuna & Chenoa
Oklahoma City

"I'm directing what we will do in Oklahoma City," Lydia announced. "I've always wanted to see the First Americans Museum." With Ellie perched atop her backpack, Lydia approached the First Americans Museum, taking in the unusual design of the building, mostly of glass and stone. They walked under a monumental arch, not unlike the one at every McDonald's. "I know so little about native peoples," Lydia said. "But I do know many, even from our own Blount County, were resettled to Oklahoma."

"This is what I learned about the museum on the internet," Eleanor said somberly. "The museum celebrates the thirty-nine tribal nations now living in the state of Oklahoma and has incorporated their culture into the architecture and exhibits. It was designed in two intersecting arcs that track the seasons as the sun changes position in the sky. True to Native American beliefs surrounding life and spirits, the exhibits in the museum do not seem to have a defined beginning or end. Different areas of the museum are filled with light during different seasons, reflecting the spiritual beliefs of native Americans about the powerful connectivity of Mother Earth and the natural world."

Lydia walked up the stone steps and entered the cool, hushed lobby. She paused to read a large plaque on the wall explaining how, in the 1830s, the U.S. government forced Native Americans off their ancestral lands. Over 15,000 people were forced to relocate to Oklahoma on the devastating journey known as the 'Trail of Tears.' Lydia felt her throat tighten; tears pricked her eyes. So much suffering, so much injustice done to these people.

Lydia wandered into the first exhibit hall, marveling at Native American artifacts and artworks surrounding them. Intricately beaded moccasins, clay pots embellished with geometric designs, tanned hides decorated with colorful paints. Each piece gave a glimpse into the incredible craftsmanship and culture of the tribes.

Lydia turned the corner into the next gallery and stopped short. Ellie almost fell from her perch on top of her backpack. Before them stood two ghostly figures—a Native American man and a Native American woman glowing with ethereal light. Though translucent, their traditional clothing and serene expressions appeared lifelike.

"It's Kanuna and Chenoa," Ellie whispered reverently. Of course, Ellie understood what was happening. The male ghost, though shimmering, stood tall with jet-black hair, deep-set eyes, and a stoic demeanor. The female ghost had long flowing hair, a beaded dress of deerskin, and a gentle, ethereal presence. She exuded compassion and calm. The ghosts regarded Lydia kindly as if they'd been expecting her.

Kanuna spoke. "O siyo Dinadala I—Hello, Sister in the Cherokee language. I am a First American from the 1800s. My name means Bullfrog, like your friend.

Eleanor's Leap

My companion, Chenoa, whose name means white dove, and I will guide you while you are in the museum. Your heart tells us you are deeply touched by our history and genuinely want to learn more about our heritage."

Lydia blinked in awe. Chenoa glided forward. "The struggles of our people must not be forgotten."

Lydia found her voice. "We want to understand. Please, tell us your history."

Then Kanuna and Chenoa guided Lydia and Ellie through the rest of the museum, explaining the people's lives, the unique cultures, and the sad histories. In one gallery, they came across an exhibit depicting the Trail of Tears. Ellie studied an informational plaque describing the harsh conditions and immense loss of life suffered by the Cherokee, Choctaw, Creek, and Chickasaw nations.

"How awful," Lydia said, her voice hushed. "Can you imagine being driven out of your homeland like that? And the people of these tribes came from where we live now." She shook her head, eyes misty. Reading the personal accounts of those who survived the brutal journey opened her heart. She thought of her own small struggles back home in Alabama. What right did she have to feel sorry for herself when others had endured such tragedy?

In the next room, vibrant works of ledger or narrative art caught Lydia's eye. The colorful drawings depicted scenes of daily Native American life—men hunting buffalo, women harvesting crops, and children playing stickball games. Despite the devastation they faced, the people in these images still expressed joy. "Look how they're smiling," Lydia said to Ellie. "Even after everything, they found ways to celebrate life."

Ellie nodded. "Their resilience is inspiring."

With each exhibit, Lydia's respect deepened. She vowed to share these stories when she returned home. The past was painful, but remembering it kept heritage alive. Kanuna spoke of his boyhood before white settlers came. "My tribe lived in harmony with nature, taking only what we needed. Game was plentiful, and we wanted for nothing."

Chenoa described her village. "We did what people do—women cooking, men crafting tools, children

Eleanor's Leap

playing. Daily life held simple joys until white soldiers arrived, bringing death and disease."

Lydia and Ellie listened in solemn silence as Chenoa continued. "You are right that our people are resilient–not just back then, but today. There are millions of our descendants still walking this earth, still speaking and teaching our beautiful languages and carrying on our traditions. Still speaking up for the more-than-human world. Still holding sacred knowledge about our ancestral homelands. Let these stories of the past be a reminder that this land and her creatures have witnessed many things and will witness many more."

The ghosts' firsthand accounts brought painful history to life in a deeply personal way. Later Lydia paused before a collection of black-and-white photographs showing Native American families standing beside their thatched-roof lodges. Their clothing and hairstyles looked so different from hers, yet their eyes held that same spark of humanity.

From her perch on Lydia's backpack, Eleanor croaked, "My ancestors were well thought of by most native American tribes. According to Native American spirituality, we frogs symbolize feminine energy, fertility, and new beginnings. And seeing one of us usually means rain is coming. We can also mean transformation. That comes from how we change from an egg to a tadpole to a four-legged frog. Maybe I can point you, Lydia, to change in your life. Come to think of it, I already have!"

Indeed! Both Lydia and Ellie left the First Americans Museum. Lydia's heart ached, but she also felt profound gratitude for the opportunity to learn about the First Americans' history, tragedy, and resilience. "That was..." Lydia struggled to find the words. "I don't think I've ever felt history so deeply before. It's like those stories are a part of me now."

Ellie nodded, her expression uncharacteristically

solemn. I'm glad we were able to listen and learn."

Lydia shook her head, processing the turmoil of her emotions—sadness for the tragedy, anger at the cruelty, and inspiration from their perseverance. Most of all, she felt profoundly grateful to the ghosts for entrusting her and Ellie with their stories. They left the museum carrying the stories of Kanuna and Chenoa in their hearts.

Ellie smiled at her friend, seeing that the visit had ignited something in Lydia—a new sense of direction, a reconnection with her own buried strength, and a perspective in life much greater than her own story.

"Where to next?" Lydia asked as they packed back into Buttercup.

"Further west. Next, to Amarillo, Texas." Ellie replied.

Chapter 10
Palo Duro Canyon
Amarillo, Texas

They woke up to the first rays of the morning sun kissing the rugged cliffs of Palo Duro Canyon, casting a warm glow over the vast landscape. It was a magnificent red and gold sunrise over the canyon. Foregoing a visit to the town of Amarillo, Lydia couldn't resist the allure of hiking a trail into Palo Duro Canyon State Park.

While she packed up camp, Ellie cheerfully chirped facts about the canyon. "Palo Duro is the second largest canyon in the country. It's at least 250 million years old, dug by the Red River on its 2,000-mile trek toward the Mississippi. And, it was the film site for *Indiana Jones and the Last Crusade*."

Lydia listened with affection. Eleanor Roosevelt was hopping with enthusiasm as she listed each fact.

Lydia, equipped with a backpack, sturdy boots, long pants, a trail map, and Eleanor atop her backpack, embarked on the journey to uncover the secrets hidden within the canyon's depths. She walked along the trails, enjoying the wildflowers and colorful rock formations. "After yesterday's intense experience in the First Americans Museum, I am so happy to spend today outdoors in nature. It feels healing."

Then, in the distance, Lydia noticed a lone figure, a silhouette against the vast canyon backdrop. A man walked toward her, tipped his hat, smiled in greeting, and introduced himself as Beau, a modern-day cowboy. He was tall and lean, and cut a striking figure against the rugged backdrop of the canyon.

His sun-kissed skin spoke of days spent under the relentless western sun. His well-worn denim jeans, scuffed cowboy boots, and a dusty brown hat that shaded his piercing blue eyes were genuine cowboy attire. Beau's eyes held the most intrigue—blue orbs dancing with mischief and confidence. They carried a glint that hinted at a certain level of cunning, leaving anyone who crossed paths with him to wonder what secrets might lie behind that charming façade.

After introducing themselves, Beau drawled, "Well, ma'am, reckon you look like a lost filly in these parts. Now, I ain't one to see a lady struggle, especially in these treacherous canyons. How 'bout I lend you a hand and guide you up the Rylander Fortress Cliff Trail? There are some mighty spectacular views from up there. But it can be a really tough hike for a loner, and I'd hate to see any harm come to such a pretty thing like yourself."

Thoughts raced through Lydia's mind. She wanted to take that trail with the scenic overlooks at the top along the canyon rim but was conflicted. Heights made her uneasy, and Beau made it sound like it could be dangerous for her to go alone. Plus, his blue eyes were so intriguing…could he be her Prince Charming?

While she was thinking, Beau moved closer. He placed a hand on her lower back as if to guide her down the trail. "Come along, little lady, let's move on down the trail now," he said in a cajoling tone.

His touch startled Lydia out of her thoughts. She sensed Eleanor Roosevelt moving around in her backpack and snapped back into her senses. She had just

Eleanor's Leap

met this man, and she didn't like being pushed. She stepped away from his hold on her waist and said, "I appreciate the offer, Beau, but I reckon I can manage just fine on my own. Folks 'round here have been kind enough to give me directions."

Beau chuckled, his eyes narrowing as he leaned closer. "Darlin', it ain't just about directions. These trails can be deceiving. I reckon you might find yourself in a spot of trouble without someone who knows the lay of the land. Besides, it gets mighty lonesome out there, and I'd enjoy the company of a charming lady like yourself."

Lydia, now more suspicious than ever, said firmly, "Well, Beau, I thank you kindly for the offer, but I'll find my own way; no need for any 'help' that might come with strings attached."

Beau grinned, his intentions laid bare, "Now, no need for suspicions, ma'am. Just trying to be a gentleman in these parts." With a tip of his hat, Beau sauntered off, leaving Lydia with a mixture of relief and caution and a trail to navigate on her own.

Ellie popped out of the backpack, "Lydia, whew, I was getting bad vibes from that guy. There was absolutely nothing prince-like about him. I'm proud of you for telling him to leave. But now you really need to go up that treacherous path."

"I'm not so sure I can do it, Ellie. I just said that trying to sound confident because I wanted to get rid of Beau. But the truth is I'm not sure that I can do it on my own. That trail goes high up, and I'm afraid of heights. I get dizzy and nauseous and picture myself tumbling over into the abyss." She pulled out a peppermint with shaking hands and popped it into her mouth.

Eleanor was adamant. They were so close to this magnificent view, and she knew how much it would mean to Lydia to conquer her fear. "Lydia, I want to give you some wisdom from my namesake, the great and courageous Eleanor Roosevelt, the first. She said, '*You must do what you think you cannot do.'* I know you can do this. You only have to prove it to yourself."

Lydia gave a resolute nod. "You're right." She gulped. "And, at least I have an encouraging frog by my side. I need to prove to myself I can do this without the need for any prince to save me."

Eleanor erupted with a little croaking cheer and hopped ahead of Lydia, skipping easily from boulder to boulder, cheering Lydia on in the more challenging moments. They climbed higher and higher on the Rylander Fortress Cliff trail. Eleanor was light on her froggy feet, but Lydia had to be careful of her footing, especially in places with loose rocks.

As the trail became narrower and more treacherous, Lydia dropped to crawl on her hands and knees, careful to avoid looking over the ledge until she could sit securely with her back against a rock.

After what seemed like an eternity of climbing, they arrived at the peak. She leaned against a large red rock, closed her eyes, and let out a big sigh. She had made it. At this point, she was too exhausted even to feel nervous about the height. She opened her eyes and looked out at the landscape. The vista spread out before her was truly amazing, fascinating rock formations — spires, and mesas in red, orange, purple, and brown hues. Below those wound an intricate network of canyons, gorges, and wrinkled riverbeds, all carved by millions of years of erosion.

"Wow," she whispered to Ellie. "I can't believe my eyes. It was worth every inch I climbed, even though I ended up having to crawl on my hands and knees to get here."

Eleanor was just as awed. "It takes my breath away. I can hardly croak…but, look," she pointed toward the valley beside them. "There's a little meadow up here…a blaze of wildflowers! Red, orange, and pink like paintbrushes. Then over there! Lupines or bluebonnets,

Eleanor's Leap

the Texas state flower. And then even more—see those yellow ones that look like daisies! It's all just dazzling!"

Lydia looked out with pride and contentment. She could never have imagined that she would be brave enough to see a view like this. She was clear once again that she hadn't needed a prince to rescue her; she had simply needed a friend to encourage her to face the things that scared her.

While Lydia was still gazing out over the canyon, Ellie started to explore the red rocks of the peak where they sat. Just to her left, she caught sight of a very ugly little creature–a small but scary-looking lizard with spiked horns all over its head. She leaned in inquisitively. "What are you? You look sort of like a frog, but not really…I've never seen anything like you. Are you dangerous?" She called out to the lizard. "Hey, you ugly creature, are you thinking of eating me?"

Eleanor jumped back in shocked surprise as a warm spray of blood shot out of the creature's eyeball. It didn't quite hit Eleanor, but it came close. She took a small hop back toward Lydia for safety.

Lydia squealed, but the creature didn't advance. She pulled her guidebook from the backpack because Eleanor looked too upset to consult the internet. "The book says this little guy is a Texas horned lizard–the official state reptile. It has many ways to avoid being eaten. Besides the horns, it can also flatten itself, and its color makes it blend into the rocks and vegetation. And, if threatened, it can shoot blood out of its eyelid as a way to frighten predators!"

"Frightened?" Eleanor scoffed. She felt bolder now that she had distanced herself from the lizard. "More like grossed out."

The lizard looked at Eleanor and Lydia. Now that Ellie had a moment to look at it, she could see that he looked more scared himself than intimidating. He couldn't have been more than five inches long, much smaller than her. He quickly confirmed her assessment with a quivering reply.

"Please excuse me. I'm not trying to eat you. I'm afraid of you eating me! I haven't seen a critter quite like you before in these parts."

Ellie looked down her nose at the creature, "Even though you are smaller than me, I certainly wouldn't want to eat something so ugly and scary. That's quite an array of horns around your head. What's with this blood coming out of your eyes?"

The lizard looked proud. "It did scare you, didn't it? This is my territory. I live here. You are welcome as long as you don't eat me."

Eleanor was about to give a scathing reply, but she noticed Lydia's disapproving look before she could get out the words. "Didn't your namesake have some thoughts about tolerance, kindness, and courage?" Chagrinned, Eleanor swallowed and changed her approach, thankful to be reminded of her strong moral fiber.

"Thank you, little creepy lizard, for welcoming us. I promise not to eat you."

The lizard gave a curt nod and scampered off between the rocks.

After a bit more time to take in the fantastic view, Lydia and Ellie headed back down the trail. Lydia's fear of heights was triggered again, but she refused to get back on her hands and knees this time. She found a walking stick and that was good enough. She focused on her breath and put one foot firmly in front of the other, keeping her eyes focused on the rocks ahead. Sooner than she expected, they reached the bottom of the trail and safely returned to Buttercup.

Lydia was proud of herself. She felt she had crossed a threshold. Hiking this trail was a major accomplishment. She could navigate her life and the transitions she faced.

Ellie was proud of Lydia and also felt triumphant—having met the Texas horned lizard and not eating it or being eaten by it.

The two adventurers left Palo Duro Canyon carrying the memories of its majestic landscapes. The canyon had become more than just a geological wonder; it had become a teacher.

Chapter 11
Hot Air Balloons in Albuquerque, New Mexico

Lydia and Eleanor arrived in Albuquerque, New Mexico, late evening. They located a vast empty field and decided to camp under the stars. The night sky was bright with moonlight and distant stars scattered like diamonds across a deep navy blue. Lydia didn't even put up the tent. She laid out the sleeping bag and put Eleanor's box beside her. Ellie hopped off to find her dinner of bugs. Lydia opened the package of hot Mexican tamales she had bought before they stopped for the night. The aroma steaming out made her mouth water. She watched the stars until her eyelids refused to stay open.

Just before dawn, they awoke to quite a hubbub. People were moving around them; lively chatter filled the previously hushed field. Eleanor hopped up immediately, feeling the excitement of the crowd. Lydia rubbed her eyes and tried to piece together what was happening. She heard a loud whooshing sound to her left, followed by the *oohs* and *ahs* of the crowd. Turning, she understood immediately what all the excitement was about.

A hot air balloon was quickly taking shape; the whooshing sound she'd heard was the propane flame

Eleanor's Leap

heating the air to fill the balloon. The flame illuminated the bright colors of the balloon, creating an effect like a giant glowing lantern. A big smile stretched across Lydia's face. Eleanor hopped with joy. What a beautiful sight!

After watching the balloon inflate to its full size, Lydia rubbed her eyes again, stretched, and looked around the field. What she saw amazed her even more–it wasn't just this one balloon. Dozens of balloons were popping up all over the field, each more brightly colored than the last. Teams of people gathered around each inflating balloon. She and Eleanor had awoken right in the middle of a hot-air balloon festival!

The sight of the balloons lighting the pre-dawn landscape was truly breathtaking. The air filled with a symphony of hissing burners and excited chatter. The anticipatory joy of balloon adventures buzzed the air. A nearby group gathered around a purple and blue balloon and began a countdown. "Five, four, three, two, one…lift off!" The balloon, released from its tether, floated gently up into the air.

Eleanor clapped her webbed hands. She thought of the dragonflies back home at the pond and how they moved so gracefully from one lily pad to the next. She wanted to fly!

As if she could read Eleanor's mind, Lydia commented, "Wow, what a wonderful experience to see all these balloons. What a treat! I wish we could take a ride, but I'm sure it's expensive. Watching will have to be enough for us."

Eleanor looked at her skeptically. "Lydia, I think you've had too many days of 'just watching.' Don't you want to fly? You don't even know how much it costs, and you're already telling yourself it's impossible."

Lydia had to admit that Eleanor had a point. "Of course, I want to fly, but how am I supposed to find a way to ride?"

"Well, sitting here isn't going to make money fall on your head," Ellie said.

Lydia eyed Eleanor as she reluctantly stood up. Ellie could be a pushy little frog sometimes. "Go ask one of these pilots. All they can say is 'no.'" Ellie prompted.

"You're right. They can only say 'no.'"

Lydia approached the nearest balloon. Its colors were warm and bright, checkered with yellows, oranges, and reds. "Excuse me, sir?" She called out, approaching the man who appeared to be in charge. "I camped here for the night and woke up to the sight of these beautiful balloons. I don't have a ticket, but I sure would love to join y'all for a ride. Is there any way I can hop in?

"Sorry, lady, my balloon is full," he replied gruffly.

Lydia's face dropped with disappointment. She knew the chances were slim, but she had gotten her hopes up. He reconsidered and gave her a questioning look and pointed at a green and teal balloon further down the field. "But Alex over there isn't full, and I heard they were down a crew member."

Lydia brightened. "Thank you so much!" Eleanor hopped into her backpack, and they headed down the field. She approached a woman in the group beside the green and teal balloon. "I'm looking for a man named Alex?" Lydia asked. "I heard his crew might need a helper on this ride?"

The woman replied with a skeptical tone. "We don't have any men named Alex here."

Lydia started to apologize, but the woman continued before Lydia could get a word out. "But I'll be piloting this balloon today and I could use another helping hand."

Lydia stood with her mouth open for a moment. The woman gave her a friendly grin and tossed her a bundle of ropes. "I'm Alexis—Alex for short. Glad to have you on board." Lydia could feel Ellie's excited squirming in her backpack. They were going flying! Lydia jumped in to assist Alex with the balloon setup and preparation. Only after they'd climbed into the basket to prepare for liftoff did Lydia remember her fear of heights.

She closed her eyes and said softly to herself, "I won't often have this opportunity in my life. I did the hike in Palo Duro yesterday, and it was high. I focused on the beauty and the sense of adventure. I did what I thought I could not do, and I can do it again today!"

Eleanor watched her friend with admiration. When Lydia opened her eyes, Eleanor could see she would be okay. "Well," she said to Lydia. "I'm not afraid of heights, but I sure don't want to fall out of the balloon."

"Don't worry," Lydia reassured her. "You can take the ride peeking out of my backpack. I won't let you fall as long as you stay put."

Ellie stayed perched atop Lydia's backpack as Alex opened the gate and began loading up a diverse group of fellow adventurers. Though they were initially surprised to be traveling along with a frog, the group soon embraced the unexpected companion. Alex confidently gave the whole group instructions, and their camaraderie grew as they took turns handling the burners. Each person soon found their position in the eight-person, one-frog balloon basket.

Just as dawn fully broke, almost a hundred hot air balloons ascended, revealing a magical sunrise over Albuquerque. The sky transformed into a canvas of pastel hues — soft pinks, oranges, and purples — casting a warm glow on the sprawling city below. The Sandia Mountains stood majestic, bathed in the first light, while the Rio Grande reflected the changing colors.

Encouraged by the supportive atmosphere, Lydia embraced the sensation of floating. Her fear of heights morphed into delight. She loved the sensation of soaring high over the hills in a balloon. She exhaled in joy. "Who could have imagined?"

Inside the balloon basket, Eleanor's presence added an element of whimsy to the balloon adventure for everyone except, Lydia noticed, one traveler who was growing increasingly uneasy. Her knuckles were white as she clutched the side of the basket; her face was pale. The other passengers were too excited by their own experience to notice this woman's eyes welling up with tears.

Ellie had noticed, too. Fearful that this could become a full panic attack, Eleanor took a risk and spoke to the traveler in a soothing voice. "Fear not, my friend. Up here, the sky is a canvas of serenity. Embrace the wind, the beauty below, and the shared joy of this adventure. Let's float together and turn your fear into a memory of courage.

"Look at my friend Lydia–she was terrified of heights just yesterday, and look at her today!" Lydia couldn't be sure if it were Eleanor's words of encouragement or simply the shock of hearing a frog speak while floating in a hot air balloon, but the woman's fear seemed to loosen its grasp as Eleanor spoke.

The rest of the passengers chimed in with their own uplifting words, and soon, she was smiling along with everyone else. Somehow, the magic of a talking bullfrog was folded into the magic of the whole experience. The consensus was that Eleanor Roosevelt was, indeed, a remarkable frog.

Lydia, Eleanor, and their companions witnessed a breathtaking panorama from the balloon's lofty vantage point. Below, the Rio Grande wound through the desert and the majestic Sandia Mountains stood with long shadows. As they ascended, other balloons dotted the sky, creating a colorful ballet. The adventurers got close to the neighboring balloons, exchanging waves and laughter with fellow sky-bound travelers.

As their balloon floated higher and away from the other balloons, the silence aloft fostered quiet introspection. Surrounded by the beauty of nature unfolding, they felt a profound connection to the universe, the sunrise a renewal, mirroring their inner transformations. Eleanor croaked rhythmically, in harmony with the world. Adventure, Lydia realized, is not merely external but a profound exploration within.

Later that afternoon, with the serene, shared revelation of the balloon ride lingering like a dream into another world, Lydia and Eleanor Roosevelt, the extraordinary bullfrog, left Albuquerque, driving toward their next destination, Flagstaff, Arizona.

Chapter 12
Sedona & the Fortune Teller

At this point in their road trip, the familiar tasks of packing camp, loading up Buttercup, and getting on the road were a comforting routine. Lydia felt herself relax into the drive, singing along to the radio as Eleanor confidently chirped occasional directions or facts about the places they passed through. Lydia loved the thrill of each adventure they had, but she also loved the hours of driving down the highway. Some people might have found that part boring, but not Lydia. She liked the feeling of simply sitting next to her friend and driving.

She was basking in this feeling when she heard Eleanor's voice take an unfamiliar tone. "Um, Lydia…." she croaked, "I'm not sure how, but I think we must have taken a wrong turn." It took a moment for Lydia to place what it was about Eleanor's tone that seemed so strange. It was doubt—that's what she was hearing! She could hardly think of another time she'd heard the extraordinary Eleanor Roosevelt express doubt.

"Don't worry, Ellie," Lydia said reassuringly. "We'll just turn back around and get back on track."

Eleanor nodded, but she wasn't totally at ease. She could usually rely on her sense of direction, but this place felt eerily hard to navigate.

Eleanor's Leap

Lydia turned Buttercup around. Strangely, Eleanor's nervousness made Lydia feel steadier. In a reversal of their usual roles, Lydia was now the calm one.

They backtracked for a while and then backtracked again. The GPS signal had faded, and the road became uneven. Dusk was coming on, and Eleanor couldn't figure out how to get them back to the main road. The silence of the wilderness was broken only by the distant howls of coyotes, adding a spooky element to the situation.

Eleanor couldn't shake her unsettled feeling. She liked wandering, but she wasn't used to feeling lost.

"How about we just set up camp for now and try again in the morning?" Lydia suggested. "There aren't many cars around here. I'm sure we can find a place to pull off and rest. Things always seem easier after a rest."

Ellie reluctantly agreed. She didn't like the feeling of this place, but they didn't seem any closer to finding their way. They unpacked for the night. They had enough food. Lydia managed to sleep well enough, but Ellie was jittery and on guard.

As Lydia predicted, the next morning dawned bright and cheerful. The landscape transformed into a surreal array of red rock formations. This place didn't seem so ominous anymore, and the air felt charged with a spiritual energy. They got back on the road and headed in the direction that felt right to Lydia, and it was only a few minutes before they saw signs of a town ahead–not Flagstaff, as they'd intended, but the mystical city of Sedona.

Though bags hung under her froggy eyes, Eleanor was back in her element, hopping with excitement in the passenger seat. "Google tells us that Sedona is a stunning town surrounded by breathtaking red rock formations in the high desert of Arizona. A landscape characterized by towering sandstone cliffs, mesas, and buttes painted in vibrant red, orange, and brown shades.

The beauty of Sedona is enhanced by its unique geological features, creating a magical and otherworldly atmosphere."

Eleanor shifted into a hushed, mysterious tone, "One of the distinctive aspects of Sedona is the presence of vortexes, which are believed to be powerful energy centers scattered throughout the region."

Lydia was relieved to hear the confidence back in Eleanor's voice. The added dramatic flair was a sign that Ellie felt like herself again.

Eleanor continued in a theatrical whisper. "These vortexes are thought to emit spiritual and healing energies, drawing people seeking tranquility, self-discovery, and a connection with nature. The vortexes are not physically visible but are said to be felt as intensified energy sensations at specific locations."

She instructed Lydia to take a few quick turns, and they arrived at Back O' Beyond Road, the trailhead of Cathedral Rock. This was one of the most famous vortex sites. As they approached the large sandstone mass, the energy felt particularly intense. A gentle breeze whispered of ancient tales, and the air shimmered with a mystical glow. There were a few marked trails; they took the one that looked the least traveled.

"There's definitely something powerful going on here," Lydia confirmed. She looked down at her arm and saw goosebumps prickling. The energy felt intense!

After a few minutes of walking among the towering red rock formations, they found an ornate tent nestled between the rocks, adorned with colorful fabrics and mystical symbols. This place was intriguing, if a bit foreboding.

Lydia was startled to notice a woman draped in flowing robes that reflected the surrounding red rocks' hues, standing right outside the tent. The woman's eyes—deep and mysterious, sparkling with otherworldly wisdom—drew Lydia in.

Eleanor's Leap

    As they approached, the woman gestured, welcoming them toward the tent with a knowing smile. "Come along, travelers," she called. "I sensed your presence before you even arrived. The energy of this vortex has brought you here for a reason. I have been awaiting your arrival. The spirits have a message for both of you."

    Lydia and Eleanor exchanged a glance—if Eleanor had had eyebrows, she would have raised them. Lydia nodded and stepped toward the fortune teller. She was learning to trust her intuition, and her intuition was telling her that this woman had some wisdom to share.

    It took them a moment to get oriented as they stepped from the sunny desert into the tent's interior. The space was filled with an eclectic mix of items, hinting at magic and mystery. Crystal balls caught the sunlight, casting prisms of color across the interior. Tarot cards were neatly arranged on a small table, and incense wafted through the air. Various trinkets and talismans were scattered on every surface, each significant, Lydia suspected.

Again, the woman seemed to blend into the surroundings, settling on a cushion behind a table set with an enticing mix of crystals and candles. She gestured at them again, her hand adorned with ornate rings that glittered in the light. Eleanor Roosevelt solemnly sat on the cushion across the table, listening with rapt attention. Lydia sat down beside her, intrigued.

"Lydia, you are a woman experiencing many changes in your life. And, though most humans are unaware, I see this unusual friend, this frog, as a creature with many gifts and much wisdom of her own."

The fortune teller smiled. "Let the energy of this vortex guide us." She looked at Lydia and then adjusted the crystals on the table. She looked at Eleanor and then shuffled a deck of tarot cards. The air was thick with anticipation. The woman muttered to herself and placed a few cards on the table. She almost looked like she was trying to solve a puzzle.

"Eleanor Roosevelt," she said, "you are no ordinary frog, of course! You're on a journey, I take it?"

Lydia watched Eleanor take a deep breath before responding. Sometimes, it was easy for her to forget that her friend was a magical creature, but at that moment, she could see that Eleanor understood some things about the world that were mysterious to a normal human like herself.

"Greetings, wise one," the frog responded. "Yes, Lydia and I are on an important journey. We've traveled from rural Alabama and are bound for Calaveras County, California, for the famous frog-jumping contest. There is a fortune to be made there if I jump best."

The fortune teller nodded and smiled, looking again at the cards she shuffled in her hands. After a moment, she lifted her gaze to Lydia. "And Lydia, I presume?

Eleanor's Leap

You are no ordinary human, traveling with this froggy companion. There is a distinct magical aura surrounding you both. Tell me more about your journey so far."

As Lydia and Eleanor shared more about their adventures, the tent became a haven where the ordinary and magical seamlessly coexisted. The fortune teller was intrigued and delighted by the details of each place they'd encountered. When their story reached their arrival at Cathedral Rock, they explained how they'd been drawn to this place. The woman nodded affirmatively.

"Cathedral Rock is a place where the veil between worlds is thin, and the universe's energies converge. Magic attracts magic. It makes sense that you would be pulled to this place. Now that you've shared your wonderful story with me, would you like a reading from me?"

They both responded at once, Eleanor Roosevelt with an enthusiastic "Yes!"

Lydia was more hesitant, "What does that mean, exactly?"

The fortune teller explained, "The spirits will guide me to share insights with you, to illuminate the path that lies ahead." She gazed deeply into her crystal ball, her fingers lightly tracing the surface as she tapped into the energies circling Lydia and Eleanor. After Lydia's affirmative nod, the fortune teller continued, her voice taking on a rhythmic and enchanting quality.

"I see a fascinating journey ahead for both of you. Ah, Lydia.... I sense a forthcoming challenge on your path. A golden opportunity will present itself, a chance to increase your fortunes in ways you may not yet imagine. Keep your eyes open and be ready to seize the moment when it arrives. This will entail a test of your courage and moral resilience. But fear not, for the key to unlocking a greater fortune lies within this challenge. Embrace the obstacles that come your way, for they are stepping stones to a prosperous future."

    Lydia shot a knowing glance at Eleanor. This was surely referencing the contest in Calaveras County, and the strength it would take to make the rest of the journey there.

    Turning her attention to Eleanor, the fortune teller continued, "Eleanor Roosevelt, the bond you share with Lydia is precious and powerful. Your friendship is a beacon of light in both of your lives." Eleanor smiled at Lydia. She knew that their friendship was special and appreciated the affirmation. Then the fortune teller continued, "However…." She trailed off for a moment.

    Eleanor fidgeted, perched on the edge of her seat. Like her namesake, Eleanor had a lot of virtues, but patience wasn't one of them. After what felt like a long pause, she prompted the fortune teller to continue. "However—?"

    "However, I see a time of testing approaching. Challenges may arise that threaten the harmony you've built together. Remember, true friendship can weather any storm. Stay true to each other, communicate openly, and your bond will emerge even stronger." The woman seemed to snap out of her trance state. She looked at them with clear eyes.

    They could see that the reading was over.

    The fortune teller looked into their eyes with a knowing smile. "The future is never set in stone, but with awareness and a shared resolve, you have the power to shape your destiny. Walk forward with confidence and may the magic of this vortex guide you on your journey."

    Lydia and Eleanor gathered themselves and left the tent, blinking their eyes. The bright sunlight was jarring after the soft candlelight of the tent. Eleanor turned back as they were about to continue down the trail. "You go on ahead, Lydia. I want to check one thing, and I'll be right behind you."

Eleanor's Leap

Lydia, still a bit dazed, nodded and continued walking. She didn't mind having a moment to reflect on what the fortune teller had said.

Eleanor hopped back into the tent. The fortune teller was still seated behind the crystal ball, unsurprised by Eleanor's return. She smiled serenely without looking up. "You have more questions, Eleanor?"

"Just one thing I had to ask about," Eleanor said. "I'm on a quest with Lydia, as you know. But I'm also on my own quest. I'm on this journey to win the frog jumping contest in Calaveras County—the Olympics of frog jumping. I want to prove to the world that I'm the best jumper there is."

The fortune teller looked back at her with knowing eyes. "Yes, Eleanor, and? What is your question?"

"Well...." Eleanor squirmed. Sedona was turning out to be a challenging place for her! "I *know* that I'm the best jumper there is, but I just thought, maybe you and those spirits could confirm...if I will win the contest? It's just that Lydia brought me all this way, and a lot is riding on this. If I don't win the contest, Lydia won't get the money she needs, and this whole trip will have been a waste."

The fortune teller looked into her crystal ball as she answered. "You are a very smart frog, but you misunderstand my gift, Eleanor Roosevelt. I am not a seer of the future in that way. You are the master of your own destiny. I cannot tell you whether or not you will win."

Eleanor couldn't hide her disappointment. "Ok then," she said, hopping down from the cushion. "Thanks, anyway, I guess."

"But—," the fortune teller said as she looked closely into the crystal ball. Eleanor bounced nervously back on her cushion. This woman loved to build suspense. "But there is more. Eleanor, even if others don't, you must know that your magic is much deeper than simply an ability to talk or use the internet. You are a magical companion—the bond that you've made with Lydia has invoked something ancient and powerful."

Eleanor wasn't sure what to make of this. She already knew there was something special in her friendship with Lydia. That's what made the contest all the more important. She didn't want to disappoint her friend.

"If what you seek is to give your friend her heart's desire, you do have greater magic to use. But, Eleanor, I must give you caution. Using this magic means giving it away."

She peered into the ball as if she were trying to read something that was blurred. "To grant this wish for your friend will cost you…everything…all of your magic. This is a gift you can only give once. After that, you will just become a normal bullfrog. No speech, no internet. No exceptional moral fiber. Just a normal frog. You understand?"

Eleanor's usual vibrance was subdued as she considered the fortune teller's words. She nodded and turned to the entrance of the tent to hop away.

"Oh, and one more thing."

Eleanor looked back. "One more phrase that keeps coming up. Eleanor, *there is more beyond.*"

Before Eleanor could get out the words to ask the woman how she knew this phrase, the fortune teller stood up and whisked her out of the tent, making it clear that this was the end of her reading for the day.

Eleanor hopped back out into the sunshine and down the path, finding Lydia perched on a flat rock near the entrance of the Cathedral Rock vortex, looking a bit skeptical now that she'd had a few minutes away from the hypnotic atmosphere of the tent. She crossed her arms and raised an eyebrow.

"Vortexes and fortune-telling? It sounds a bit…mystical, doesn't it? Do you really think there's something to it?"

Eleanor's Leap

Eleanor's response was quiet, almost hesitant, unlike her usual bluster. "Lydia, I'm not sure what to make of it either, but it does ask us to be wary and pay attention to what happens next. What happens next may give us an adventure not of our liking."

As they continued their debate, Lydia couldn't shake a subtle nervousness about the upcoming challenge foretold by the fortune teller. "What if there's truth to what she said? What if our friendship is truly going to be tested?"

Eleanor placed a comforting webbed hand on Lydia's shoulder. "Challenges are a part of any journey. It's how we face them together that matters. We've overcome so much already. I believe in our friendship, and I believe in us."

Lydia looked at Eleanor, a mixture of uncertainty and determination in her eyes. "You're right. Of course, you're right, Ellie. Anyway, what did you go back to ask? Did you learn anything more about what's coming up for us?"

Eleanor shifted uneasily. "Oh, it was nothing," she replied breezily, "Just wanted to ask about some magical cure for warts this old toad in Locust Fork was always going on about. She confirmed it was a bunch of nonsense, as I suspected."

Lydia started to ask more, but Eleanor had hopped up and was heading down the path. Lydia quickly collected her things and hurried to catch up. By the time they reached Buttercup, she had forgotten her next question, returning her thoughts to the fortune teller's predictions for her own unfolding journey.

They left Cathedral Rock a bit unsettled, though not admitting it to each other.

Later, as night fell, the stars twinkled overhead, and the red rocks took on an ethereal glow. They set up camp on the edge of Sedona.

In the morning, they woke to another beautiful

sunrise. This unplanned detour had turned into a serendipitous adventure. Mystical and spiritual wonders, Lydia mused, can be found in unexpected places.

Chapter 13
The Challenge of Las Vegas

As Eleanor Roosevelt and Lydia approached Las Vegas after nightfall, the city emerged on the horizon like a sparkling mirage. The neon lights of the famous Las Vegas Strip became visible from a distance, creating a mesmerizing glow against the dark desert sky.

They tucked Buttercup away in a hotel parking lot and made their way onto the Strip. Eleanor was perched on Lydia's shoulder as they walked, occasionally commenting on the strange wonder of the scene unfolding before them. "This city is surreal! Where are we? This place is nothing like Locust Fork, that's for sure. This isn't like any place we've been before."

Lydia agreed. Her eyes could barely take in all of the lights and activity. "One thing is more astounding than the next—a massive gold Lion over here at the MGM Casino; there's the Eiffel Tower; I thought it was supposed to be in Paris; the Statue of Liberty; the Brooklyn Bridge; a rollercoaster weaving around the buildings; the Bellagio resort with the water fountains and a botanical garden. It is a city of fantasy. I never imagined coming here. So many people, such a diversity of people, young, old, American, and from everywhere. Where do we go first?"

Following the flow of the people around them, they approached the entrance to the Bellagio, one of the casinos. The fountains in front burst into a captivating display of water, lights, and music—a grand welcome to this world-renowned resort. The exterior of the Bellagio was elegant and sophisticated, a design that promised luxury and fantasy awaited inside.

Stepping through the doors, Eleanor and Lydia found themselves in a vast and opulent lobby adorned with art and floral displays. The high ceiling was a masterpiece with huge glass flowers, done by a famous glass artist. The expansive casino floor featured a wide array of gaming options, from classic table games to state-of-the-art slot machines. The atmosphere was charged with excitement as the sounds of slot machines, cheers from the tables, and the occasional ripple of laughter filled the air.

Eleanor looked around with wide eyes, her mouth open in disbelief. She loved a striking spectacle as much as anyone, but this scene disturbed her. This was an unreal world meant to hypnotize humans. In Eleanor's estimation, humans are already prone to disconnection from the real world—unaware of the plants, water, weather, and bugs. They think of themselves as separate from the natural world, even though that was clearly absurd. This place was a further extension of that, designed to make humans think of existence in an unreal way. What really mattered didn't matter here. Only fantasy seemed to matter here, make-believe.

Lydia was, thankfully, an exception to this human inclination for disconnection, Eleanor thought. She'll probably be ready to get out of here and back to Buttercup quickly. Eleanor was about to suggest this to Lydia when a casino host approached. She quickly dove into Lydia's backpack to avoid any encounter with him. The last thing she wanted in a place like this was to be made into a spectacle herself.

Eleanor listened from the safety of the backpack as the casino host introduced himself to Lydia. "Hello

Eleanor's Leap

there! I'm Sam. Are you new to Las Vegas or just the Bellagio?"

"New to the whole experience!"

"I detect a southern drawl! Where are you from?"

"Alabama. On my way to Calaveras County, California, to the frog-jumping festival. Have you heard of it?"

"I have not," Sam said. "But glad you've decided to stop over in Las Vegas. I'm here to help if you have questions. There are many ways to have fun in Las Vegas: gambling, watching shows, eating great food, and much more. Let me tell you about our brand-new slot machines, the one-armed bandits. These babies are state-of-the-art and designed to give you an unforgettable gaming experience."

Eleanor peeked out from the backpack to take a look at the machines. She was reminded of the fishing lures she would find at the bottom of the pond back home — shiny and sparkling, designed to catch attention. Even an ordinary bullfrog knew to be skeptical of something so vibrant and flashy, but judging by the rows of people whose eyes were locked on the flashing screens, ordinary humans weren't so wary.

Sam continued, "Each of the slot machines is unique. Each one tells a story. This one, for example, Lost City Treasures, is adorned with intricate details resembling an ancient, mysterious city. The reels that spin feature symbols like ancient artifacts, treasure maps, and exotic creatures. There is even background music to add to the sense of adventure."

"Why are they called 'one-armed bandits'?"

Sam chuckled. "The 'one-armed' part of the nickname refers to the traditional design of these machines, which features a lever or arm on the side. Players pull this lever to set the reels in motion. The machines are operated by inserting a coin and pulling the lever with one hand, hence the term 'one-armed.'

"And bandit? Well, that's because some folks tend to stay at the slots too long, aren't smart, and lose too much money." He looked over at Lydia with confident eyes. "If I were a betting man, I'd just bet that a sensible traveler like yourself doesn't have to worry about something like that—you deserve to loosen up now and then and have some fun, right?"

He moved closer to the machine. "Let me tell you more about this one, 'Lost City,' because there are more bonus rounds and some thrilling surprises as you unlock special features during your gameplay. It could be free spins, multipliers, or even a chance to play mini-games for extra rewards. The element of surprise adds a layer of excitement. It's all in good fun!"

Lydia opened her mouth to speak, but the man kept going.

"And what could be more fun than winning lots of money? You like money, right? Let me tell you how these jackpots work. Each machine is linked to a progressive jackpot network, meaning the potential winnings can reach astronomical amounts. The jackpot grows with every spin across the network, offering you the chance to hit it big with just a single lucky spin."

Eleanor didn't need to poke her head out to realize that Sam could see Lydia's interest growing.

"How about I'll get you started as a token of welcome on your travels? Here's a five-dollar coin on the house. Now you've got nothing to lose." Sam winked as he handed Lydia the coin. "Good luck and enjoy your time at the casino!" He backed away, giving Lydia space to choose a machine to play.

Lydia wanted to be skeptical, but it did seem like she had nothing to lose. She liked the look of that Lost City machine Sam had pointed out. She put the coin in the machine and pulled the lever.

Whirr…cling, cling, cling….

Like magic, each row fell into place with clicks and

bells. *Ding ding ding* — winner! Fifty dollars!

Lydia felt a thrill. She was a winner! And so quickly. She had never won anything before. Maybe luck was on her side today....

Eleanor Roosevelt peeked out from the backpack. She could see that Lydia was pleased, but Eleanor had a bad feeling about this. She decided to take a logical approach to slowing Lydia down. "Lydia, winning at slot machines is strictly based on luck, as these games use random number generators to determine the outcome of each spin. You won this time, but that doesn't predict what will happen next. And clearly, these casinos aren't in the business of losing money, so everyone can't win all the time."

"I understand, Ellie. Really, I do. But that was harmless fun like Sam said. I'll just play with the fifty dollars we've already won."

She put ten coins in the same machine, but this time she came up empty, with no winning combination. Eleanor could see that Lydia was disappointed. Lydia even seemed slightly surprised that she'd lost, even though she had seemed to understand that this was how these machines were designed to work.

Just as Eleanor was about to suggest that they cut their losses and head back to Buttercup, Sam reappeared, sending Eleanor back down into the depths of the backpack. *Suspiciously good timing on his part,* Eleanor thought to herself.

"How's it going over here? Having fun yet?"

"I won on my first pull but not on my second. Maybe I should back off."

Sam's voice took a comforting tone. "Every pull of the arm is different. You might win next time. Don't let it get you down. This is Las Vegas — no place to get discouraged. How about a drink and a good meal?"

Lydia was flattered. He was being so nice to her. And now that he mentioned it, she was hungry.

"Come on–it's on the house! Nothing to lose!" he said with a smile.

"Okay, okay," Lydia returned Sam's smile and accepted a ticket for a drink and a meal. "I guess there really is nothing to lose."

"That's the spirit! And, hey, we don't do this for everyone, but since you've come so far…. How about we set you up with a free room for the night? We've got a special promotion going. I can even give you some free play credits. Come on, what could be wrong with a little more harmless fun!"

Inside the backpack, Eleanor rolled her eyes. Harmless fun? Was he trying to seduce Lydia into gambling? This was just too much.

Eleanor could hardly believe Lydia's response, which could only be described as a girlish giggle.

"I guess it would be nice to stay inside such a beautiful place for the night. We don't have places like this back in Alabama."

Lydia's Southern accent sounded thicker than usual. *Oh, here we go*, Eleanor thought to herself. Lydia is buying all of this… hook, line, and sinker, just like a fish from the pond.

Lydia accepted Sam's arrangements and played the slot machines throughout the evening. Eleanor wouldn't exactly call this harmless fun, but she could see that Lydia was in a dazzled state, intoxicated by the attention she received and the energy of the place. Eleanor decided not to intervene unless things got too out of hand. After all, it was just one night, and then they'd be back on the road to Calaveras County.

After a few hours, she reached up and tapped Lydia on the arm. This was a later night than usual, and Eleanor was ready to get out of this backpack and turn in for the night. Lydia reluctantly agreed. She'd won some and then lost some throughout the night, but at this point, she had a little more money in her pocket than when she'd started.

Eleanor's Leap

The room Sam had arranged had a window facing the magnificent fountain. Lydia stood by the window and looked at the brilliant city lights. Eleanor swam a few laps around in the opulent jacuzzi, grateful to be out of all the noise and activity of the casino. After a while, she hopped out of the tub and curled up to sleep, tired after a long day. Before she closed her eyes, she saw that Lydia was still standing by the window, deep in thought. Eleanor drifted off to sleep.

Eleanor Roosevelt was usually the earlier riser, but when she opened her eyes that morning, Lydia had already been down to the buffet for coffee and breakfast and back to the room. She fidgeted anxiously while Eleanor did her morning stretches. Eleanor couldn't wait to get out of this place. She didn't like the effect it was having on her friend.

"Alright," she said as she finished up her routine. "Let's go find Buttercup and get back on the road." She could see that Lydia was hesitant.

"Ellie, I've been thinking," Lydia started.

Eleanor cut her off. "Lydia, I know this place is comfortable and fun for you as a human, but we've got a contest to win, you know?"

"That's what I've been thinking about, Ellie," Lydia continued. "I think I may have put too much pressure on this contest idea. What if we get there and the competition is too stiff? Did you know that almost 40,000 people attend this festival? And I understand hundreds of frogs are brought to compete. What if there are frogs that have been bred for this, training their whole lives?"

Eleanor was surprised. They had met some challenges on the way, but this was the first time Lydia had expressed this kind of doubt. She tried to reassure her. "I mean, I've never met a frog from California, but I'm the best jumper in one of the biggest ponds in all of Locust Fork…." Her voice faltered as she continued. "It's a pretty big pond by our county standards."

Lydia's doubt sparked Eleanor's own spiral of negative thoughts. What if she wasn't the best jumper after all? After all, the world was turning out to be a bigger place than she'd ever realized. What if they had come all this way just to lose? What would Lydia do next without the money from the contest?

As if she could read Eleanor's thoughts, Lydia moved her hand to pat Eleanor's front hand. "It wasn't fair of me to put so much pressure on you winning the contest, Ellie. That was my fault. But I've been thinking about it, and think I have a plan. I think it would be much easier to win the money I need here, at this casino! This must be the golden opportunity the fortune teller was talking about. And then we could go on to the contest as we've planned, but we wouldn't have to worry whether you would win or lose. Our problems will be solved!"

Eleanor took a moment to process. It would still matter to her whether she won or lost. She wanted Lydia to have the money, but she also wanted to win. And anyway, this was gambling. It wasn't a sure thing.

"But Lydia," Eleanor shook her head. "It's like we talked about yesterday. These machines run on random algorithms. There's no way to guarantee that you would win."

"That's what I knew you would say," Lydia replied. "But, Eleanor, what if it wasn't just random? What if you used your magic to help me win the money we need?"

"Lydia, my magic doesn't work like that. I have the power to talk and search the web. I've never even tried any other kind of magic." Eleanor paused.

"Well, that's not exactly true. In the early days in Locust Fork and after meeting you with that close call of a kiss, I remembered that the fairy godmother in the Cinderella story was able to enlist the help of mice and birds to aid Cinderella. I tried that, tried to enchant the

Eleanor's Leap

dragonflies, fish, and a few birds at your pond. But nothing happened. They all just stared at me, dumbfounded, like I was being silly." She shook her head at the memory of the smug dragonflies.

"Anyway," she continued, "that's not the point. The point is that I don't have the ability to rig a slot machine!"

Lydia begged. "Ellie, I've seen how magical things happen around you. Aren't you even willing to try? Think about what we could do with the money we could win! It wouldn't just have to be enough to get by — it could be enough money to make us rich forever. We could win a whole fortune!"

The word 'fortune' was like a trigger for Eleanor's memory. In her mind, she heard an echo from the mystical tent at Cathedral Rock, "*If what you seek is to give your friend her heart's desire, you do have greater magic to use. But this will be your last act of magic.*"

She looked at Lydia's pleading face. She knew how much Lydia needed money to keep the little house in Locust Fork, and she didn't want to disappoint her. If there was anyone in the world who should have their heart's truest desire, it was Lydia.

Lydia had her hands folded like she was praying. "Please, Ellie?"

Eleanor Roosevelt considered the consequences, a tiny tear about to drop from her eye. She loved her life as an extraordinary bullfrog. But she also loved her friend. The fortune teller had called Eleanor a magical companion. Didn't that mean she was supposed to put Lydia first?

Eleanor looked one more time into Lydia's eyes. She could see how badly Lydia wanted this, how much relief it would give her not to be worried about money or the future. If this was the life that Lydia wanted, Eleanor didn't want to stand in her way.

She scribbled words of incantation on a slip of paper.

She wasn't sure how she knew what to do; it must be ancient magic, as the fortune teller said. She handed Lydia the paper and instructed her to read the words right before she pulled the lever on the slot machine.

> *Spinning reels align for me;*
> *Bring the treasures I long to see.*
> *With each turn, let fortune flow.*
> *In Vegas lights, my winnings grow.*
> *Luck and chance, be on my side.*
> *Guide my hand as I decide.*
> *One more try, with hope so bright,*
> *Grant me fortune on this night.*

"Lydia, this will make the dearest desire of your heart come true. You'll be rich with no money worries for the rest of your days."

Lydia clapped her hands together and kissed Eleanor on her head.

"Hey, hey," Eleanor reminded her. "Still not a prince here. Just a regular ol' extraordinary bullfrog."

Lydia paused, noticing the sadness in Eleanor's voice as she said the last phrase. But before Lydia could ask any further, Eleanor rushed her along. "You go get that money and change your life, Lydia. I'll meet you back at Buttercup, and we'll all be on our way."

Eleanor wasn't sure why she didn't want to tell her friend about the consequences of giving away her magic. She had believed she could win Lydia that money in the frog jumping contest, but maybe Lydia's doubts were true. If Lydia didn't believe in her, perhaps she wasn't worth believing in. And if she couldn't even help a friend in need, what good were her magical powers, anyway? Might as well just spend the rest of her days eating bugs and floating in the pond. At least Lydia would be able to have a good life.

"Thank you so much, Ellie," Lydia said brightly.

Eleanor's Leap

"This will make my life so much easier. And I promise to always take good care of you. After I do this, we'll get back on the road worry-free. I'll meet you back at Buttercup. Here I go, back to the Lost City Treasures slot machine!"

Eleanor Roosevelt hopped down the Las Vegas Strip, soaking up her last hours as a magical bullfrog, reading all the signs and singing to herself. She was sad but also pleased that she could give this gift to her friend. She sighed. She probably wouldn't be able to win that contest now, but, she supposed, it didn't really matter. From now on, she would just be an ordinary bullfrog.

—

Not long after, Lydia hurried down the same path Eleanor had hopped that afternoon. She was relieved when she got to the parking lot where they'd stashed Buttercup. She was even more relieved to see Eleanor perched on her box in the passenger seat.

"There you are, Ellie. We can leave now. I feel wonderful. I'm happy to see you back in your box. We can head on to our next destination."

But there was no response from Eleanor.

Lydia looked puzzled. "I never saw such a sad-looking frog! Why aren't you answering me?"

Eleanor stared glumly out the passenger window.

"Eleanor Roosevelt, did you hear me? I asked you a question."

Still, no reaction.

Lydia, getting desperate, pleaded, "What do I need to do to get your attention, to listen to me? Maybe scoop you up and kiss you, like in the very beginning!"

Finally, a response from an exasperated Eleanor. "No! No! Not that! No lipstick on my beautiful amphibian skin!"

"Wait," Eleanor said, looking around in confusion. "What's this? I'm talking. How can that be? I'm not supposed to be able to talk anymore."

"Why is that?" Lydia asked, relieved that Eleanor had finally answered.

"Because," Eleanor explained; "I granted your wish of being able to make a really big win out here. The fortune teller told me that granting a wish like that would be my last act of magic. At this point, I'm just your average, run-of-the-mill frog."

Lydia took a moment to process Eleanor's words. Tears sprung up in her eyes as she realized the sacrifice her friend had been willing to make for her. She really was lucky, even if it wasn't in the way she had thought in the casino.

"First of all, Eleanor Roosevelt, you could never be just an average frog. And second of all — I didn't use the incantation you gave me. I didn't win any money."

Eleanor felt a weight lift from her body. She was still herself! What a relief to still be a magical frog! "But why," she looked at Lydia. "Why not?"

"Eleanor, I didn't know the sacrifice you were making for me, but I could see the slump in your shoulders as you hopped away from the casino. I thought about how confident you've been in your ability to win the jumping contest. I thought about how my new plan was based on doubting you and giving in to fear about money and the future. I don't want to be the reason that you doubt yourself, Ellie. You are my best friend, and I believe in you. I believe that you will win."

Now it was Eleanor's turn to blink back tears.

"But, Lydia," Eleanor responded. "Even if I am confident, the truth is that I don't know for sure that I will win. What if I'm not the world's best jumper?"

"Ellie, if this were a sure thing, then it wouldn't really take any courage. Courage means showing up to do your best even when you don't know how things will end."

"And what if we don't win any money?"

"The money would be nice," she admitted, "but I am

learning from this trip that I don't need money to have a good life. What I need to have a good life is a good friend, a willingness to try things, and to trust myself. I have a good friend in you, and I'm also learning to believe in myself."

Lydia cranked up Buttercup and shifted her into gear. "We don't need a big win here in Las Vegas. We can take our chances in Calaveras County."

Eleanor hopped up and down, big jumps, joy bubbling up in her heart. "I'm still a magical frog! I can still talk and search the Web! I'm the best jumper in all the land. And I still have my best friend."

Chapter 14
Bears, Fire, and Painting a Sunrise in Yosemite National Park

Lydia and Eleanor arrived in Yosemite National Park, greeted by sunlight peeking through the needles of the towering, cathedral-like sequoia trees and filtering down to cast dappled patterns on the forest floor. The air was crisp and clean, filled with the scent of pine and damp earth. Before them, Bridalveil Fall cascaded down a sheer cliff face. A rainbow arched across the mist, adding a touch of magic to the scene. It was like stepping into a fairytale.

With her keen, froggy eyes, Eleanor spotted a spiderweb shimmering with dewdrops, a family of deer grazing peacefully, and a butterfly with wings resembling stained glass.

Lydia gazed up at the towering trees, the rushing Merced River, and the vibrant wildflowers carpeting the meadows. "This is so beautiful," Lydia whispered, her voice filled with awe. "Just imagine the stories these ancient sequoias could tell."

Eleanor's Leap

Eleanor hopped closer, her big eyes reflecting the wonder of the moment. "They've seen so much, haven't they? Maybe even the dinosaurs themselves!"

Lydia knelt, gently tracing the grooves in the ancient bark. "Not quite that long, Eleanor," she chuckled. "But they've witnessed the rise and fall of empires, the changing seasons, the ebb and flow of life." These ancient trees felt like an antidote to Las Vegas.

Squirrels with their tails like bushy flags scampered along branches, chattering warnings. A deer, its coat the color of autumn leaves, emerged from the undergrowth, liquid brown eyes locking with Lydia's before it melted back into the shadows.

Reaching the valley floor, Lydia waded into the icy Merced River, the cold water swirling around her ankles. Eleanor dipped a webbed foot in and retracted it with a comical squeak.

"Too cold for a frog, I see?" Lydia teased, a smile crinkling the corners of her eyes.

As they followed a narrow trail through a dense thicket, Eleanor suddenly let out a warning croak. Lydia froze, her eyes widening as she spotted a black bear with two playful cubs just ahead. Sensing their presence, the mama bear stood on her hind legs, her gaze fixed on them.

Eleanor felt her frog knees start to shake. "I remember reading that staying calm is crucial in times like this," she said, trying to hide the tremor in her voice.

Lydia whispered, "We need to show them we mean no harm. I read somewhere we should not turn around but slowly back away."

With Lydia's words, Eleanor found some courage. In a moment of either bravery or foolishness, Eleanor hopped out in front of the bear cubs, putting on a hopping show.

Instead of being scared, the cubs were mesmerized by her antics. Seeing only a frog cavorting around, the mama bear seemed to relax a little.

Taking advantage of the distraction, Lydia spoke softly to the bears, assuring them that they were just visitors passing through. She took several slow, backward steps away from the cubs as she spoke.

The bear cubs couldn't resist playfully batting at Eleanor as she continued her little jig. The mother bear behaved as if she understood Lydia's words and allowed her to retreat. The cubs followed Eleanor a short distance before returning to their mother.

It took a few minutes of walking before Lydia felt settled enough to breathe a sigh of relief.

"Ellie," she said. "That was terrifying! I thought I was going to lose it!"

Eleanor looked surprised. "Really? You seemed so calm. I thought I was the one who was losing it."

"You?" Now, it was Lydia's turn to sound surprised. "You seemed so confident. I was worried sick that one of

Eleanor's Leap

those cubs would eat you for a snack."

"I was shaking on the inside, but I remembered a lesson from playing with the other tadpoles in the pond—a little bit of silliness goes a long way, no matter what species you're dealing with!"

After hiking for a few more hours, they decided to camp at the Upper Pines Campground. Lydia transformed the campsite into a cozy haven nestled amongst the towering pines. Eleanor hopped out of Lydia's backpack, eager to explore. As dusk painted the valley in hues of orange and purple, they gathered fallen branches for a campfire.

Nightfall brought a symphony of sounds: the rustling of leaves whispering secrets in the breeze, and the distant hoot of an owl. Later, Lydia and Eleanor joined fellow campers around a larger fire. The crackling flames created a warm sense of community.

Laughter mingled with the sizzling of marshmallows roasting over the embers, and the strumming of guitars filled the air with gentle melodies. Lydia was coaxed into playing her guitar. Her voice, clear and strong, filled the night with the iconic Bob Dylan lyrics of "Blowin' in the Wind."

> *How many roads must a man walk down,*
> *before they call him a man?*
> *How many times must a white dove sail before*
> *she sleeps in the sand?*
> *The answer, my friend, is blowing in the wind,*
> *the answer is blowing in the wind....*
> *(Blowing in the Wind* by Bob Dylan, 1963)

As the embers dwindled and the stars emerged in all their glory, the group slowly dispersed, their laughter echoing through the silent trees. Lydia and Eleanor curled up in their tent. The rhythmic chirping of crickets lulled them both into a peaceful sleep.

Sometime past midnight, Eleanor was jolted awake by a pungent smell of smoke and the unsettling crackle of flames. Panic surged through her as she leaped onto Lydia's face, her insistent croaks urging Lydia awake. "Lydia! Wake up, fire!"

Lydia's eyes snapped open. "What? Where?"

"Outside! The campfire! It's out of control!" Lydia scrambled towards the tent flap, her heart hammering a frantic rhythm. What they saw as they peered out from the tent was a nightmare come to life. Flames danced around the smoldering remains of the group campfire, their tendrils reaching out hungrily toward the surrounding trees. The once peaceful campground was now a cacophony of shouts and panicked scrambling.

"We need to make sure everyone is awake," Lydia said, her voice tight and urgent. Eleanor shot out of the tent, the cool night air a stark contrast to the fire just yards away. Her gaze darted around and landed on a young camper, frozen in terror near the blaze. Without hesitation, Eleanor hopped towards him.

"Hey! You alright?" she croaked, her voice surprisingly steady despite the tremor in her legs.

The boy, no older than ten, stumbled back, his eyes wide with fear and disbelief. "A talking frog?" he stammered, his voice barely a whisper.

"No time to explain," Eleanor rasped with urgency. "This is dangerous. You get back with your parents quickly." The boy nodded mutely and then ran away, putting a safer distance between himself and the flames.

One by one, bleary-eyed campers emerged from their tents, their faces etched with confusion and growing alarm. As the reality of the situation dawned on them, they erupted into action.

"We need water!" someone shouted. A group of campers formed a human chain, lugging buckets filled with water from the nearby Merced River. Lydia joined the line, passing bucket after bucket to splash onto the flames. Others worked in a desperate frenzy to clear away vegetation, creating a firebreak to halt the fire's advance. The once starlit sky was now ablaze with the orange glow of the wildfire, casting an unsettling light on their determined efforts—the wail of approaching sirens sliced through the smoky air. Park rangers and firefighters arrived on the scene; their swift response was a welcome sight.

At first the fire seemed to fight back, crackling and spitting embers in defiance. But slowly, with each bucket of water and swipe of a makeshift broom, the flames lost their momentum. Eleanor darted between the legs of the campers, her voice hoarse but determined. "Keep going! We can do this!"

The combined efforts of the campers and the swift response of park rangers proved to be the turning point. After what felt like an eternity, the flames finally surrendered, leaving behind a smoldering reminder of the night's ordeal.

As they watched the last embers flicker and die, relief washed over the campground. Lydia slumped beside her tired companion, "We did it, Eleanor, we got the fire out," she whispered, her voice thick with emotion. Exhausted but relieved, all the campers gathered around the smoldering remains.

Thankfully, due to their collective efforts, the fire had been contained before causing significant damage. Park rangers showed up, and several of them commended the campers for their bravery, teamwork, and quick thinking. One ranger was sterner, giving the crowd a firm lecture on campfire safety.

Though it wasn't yet dawn, the campsite bustled with activity. No one could go back to sleep after all that action. People were packing their tents, their faces etched with exhaustion and relief. The harrowing experience was a stark reminder of the delicate balance between the enjoyment of nature and the need for thoughtful caution to make sure the natural wonders of this unique park were preserved.

Lydia and Eleanor decided to go to a high place to watch the sunrise over Yosemite before leaving. They packed up Buttercup and set out for Glacier Point while it was still dark, an iconic viewpoint known for its spectacular vistas. They parked at the base of the trail, Lydia put her paints into her backpack and they started up the trail.

The crisp mountain air nipped at their skin as they ascended. The only sounds were the crunch of gravel beneath Lydia's feet and the distant hoot of an owl. As they reached the viewpoint, a gasp escaped Eleanor's throat. The panorama that unfolded before them was nothing short of breathtaking. The granite giants of the Sierra Nevada mountains stood against the inky canvas of the night sky, their peaks dusted with a faint luminescence. The valley below lay silent, a tapestry of dark greens and blacks, punctuated by the occasional twinkle of a distant star.

Then, the first blush of dawn peeked over the horizon, painting the eastern sky in soft hues of pink and orange. The transformation was mesmerizing. Once shrouded in shadow, the granite cliffs gradually revealed their majestic forms, bathed in the rising sun's warm glow. The air was crisp. The only sounds were the whispers of the wind and the distant calls of waking birds.

Half Dome, the iconic monolith, emerged from the darkness, casting a dramatic silhouette over the valley below. The surrounding peaks, shrouded in mist moments ago, now shimmered in a golden light, their valleys and meadows awakening to a new day.

Unable to contain her excitement, Eleanor hopped onto a nearby rock. The world around her was a symphony of color and light, a breathtaking display of nature's artistry.

Eleanor's Leap

Lydia stood transfixed, equally captivated by the spectacle. Her artist's soul yearned to capture the beauty on canvas. She got out her paints and began painting. It was magical. She followed the light, adding color when it appeared. She didn't worry about what was real or abstract. She only followed the color in the sky. With swift strokes, she began translating the scene onto her canvas, her brush following the dance of light and shadow across the landscape. The colors intensified as the sun rose, painting the valley in a kaleidoscope of hues. The vibrant greens of the meadows contrasted with the stark whites of the granite cliffs, while Bridalveil Fall shimmered like a cascading ribbon of diamonds.

Lydia stood in awe as the sun continued its ascent. The colors intensified, creating a breathtaking display of nature's artistry. She quickly completed one painting after another.

Ellie hopped to a nearby boulder to watch. She could hardly follow Lydia's hands, they moved so quickly. Her paintings seemed to come alive under the morning sun. Each brushstroke captured a fleeting moment, a unique perspective of the unfolding panorama. And in some paintings, nestled amongst the majestic scenery, one could see a tiny green frog. Eleanor croaked appreciatively at the tiny green figure, a subtle nod to their shared experience and friendship.

Glacier Point had reinforced in Lydia and Eleanor a profound appreciation for the cycles of nature, the beauty of Yosemite's landscapes, and the significance of embracing moments of tranquility and wonder. A near tragedy and great beauty had marked the amazing day, and now it was time to leave. Lydia packed up Buttercup with her new stack of paintings and they headed out for Angels Camp and Calaveras County, California.

Chapter 15
Angels Camp & the History of the Frog Jumping Contest

After spending the night in a campground in the rolling foothills of California's Gold Country near the quaint Gold Rush town of Angels Camp, Lydia and Eleanor excitedly approached the Calaveras County Frog Jumping Festival. They could hardly believe they'd finally made it to their destination. But arriving was overwhelming. There were thousands of people heading into the festival.

"I remember the basic Mark Twain story," Lydia said, "but forget the details. How did this festival even start?"

Happy to show off her research, Eleanor Roosevelt explained, "Mark Twain came along at the tail end of the Gold Rush. Twenty-nine years old and still known as Samuel Clemens. He was deeply in debt, having been fired from one too many newspaper jobs, and was fleeing the Civil War in the South. He was staying with a friend, hoping to find a change in luck and perhaps a pocket full of gold like so many others. He didn't find gold, but he did strike it rich in Angels Camp when he overheard a local bartender *butchering* what could have

Eleanor's Leap

been a hilarious story about one of these informal frog jumping competitions. Samuel Clemens thought to himself, I can do better than that! And the rest was history."

Lydia chuckled and asked, "Eleanor, do you know the whole story?"

"Of course, and here's how it goes: Jim Smiley was the old miner who started the whole frog-jumping idea. He loved to gamble and would offer to bet on anything and everything, from horse races to dogfights to the health of the local parson's wife. Jim caught a frog, named it Dan'l Webster and spent three months training it to jump. Then, when a stranger visited the camp, Jim offered to bet $40 that his frog could out-jump any other frog in Calaveras County. The stranger said he would take the bet if he had a frog, so Jim went out to catch one, leaving the stranger alone with Dan'l.

While Jim was away, the stranger poured lead shot down Dan'l's throat. When Jim returned with a frog for the stranger, he and the stranger set their frogs down and let them loose. The stranger's frog jumped away while Dan'l didn't budge, and the surprised and disgusted Jim paid the $40 wager. After the stranger departed, Jim noticed Dan'l's sluggishness and picked it up, finding it much heavier than he remembered. When Dan'l belched out a double handful of lead shot, Jim realized that he had been cheated and chased after the stranger but never caught him.``

"Well, that was a pretty mean trick!" Lydia said. "So, that's the story. But how about the festival today?"

"It's a four-day event and a big deal. It happens at the end of May, and between 30,000 to 40,000 people attend, bringing several hundred frogs from all over the country!"

Eleanor continued, "In 1928, the local residents initiated an annual county fair after the first road paving in Angels Camp. Many of these residents, who still had connections with Mark Twain, felt inspired to add the historic and auspicious frog jumping event, making this the first international frog jumping contest. Thus, my comment on our first day together about this event being the Olympics of frog-jumping."

Lydia excitedly added, "And I read there is much more! Contests, performances, fun fattening things to eat, carnival rides, music, goofy competitions, clothing to buy for people and frogs, a rodeo, and opportunities to sample local wines."

Eleanor said, "I understand that the actual frog jumping competition takes place in two side-by-side locations at the fairgrounds known as Frogtown. The Main Stage is where the competition takes place, and the smaller Lily Pad stage is for practicing without the pressure of competition. We'll want to start there."

Chapter 16
Eleanor & the Rodeo

"We have a few days before the frog jumping contest, so let's see what this festival is all about. I've never been to a rodeo," Lydia said as she and Eleanor wove through the crowd, taking in the sights and sounds of the festival. There was a palpable sense of excitement as people anticipated the upcoming rodeo events.

"I've checked out rodeos on the internet," Eleanor said. "The jockey just needs to ride the bull."

"Well," Lydia said, "I might be a 'frog jockey,' but I'm not riding any bull!"

"Then I guess it's up to me." Eleanor Roosevelt seemed to be caught up in the moment's energy. Spotting the rodeo arena with its corralled bulls, she became intrigued by the commotion and managed to hop over the edge of the ring into the arena. Lydia watched with concern and amusement while Eleanor made her way closer to one of the bulls. And in a daring display of enthusiasm, she jumped on the bull's back. Curious about its uninvited amphibian rider, the bull snorted and shifted its weight.

Lydia's hand flew to her mouth.

As Lydia's sidekick attempted to ride a bull at the Calaveras County Rodeo, chaos and hilarity ensued.

The bull, likely confused by the unusual rider, started bucking and jumping, trying to get the frog off its back. Then, the bull seemed to take a few steps that looked like ballet moves. The audience burst into laughter at the absurdity of a frog riding a bull trying to ballet dance.

    The rodeo announcer's voice came over the loudspeaker, "Folks, this is an unexpected event. We've got ourselves a froggy surprise in the ring tonight! Looks like that bull is feeling a little jumpy, and who can blame him with our special guest hitching a ride. Not every day do you see a bull and a bullfrog teaming up for the ultimate impromptu rodeo adventure! Will our amphibious amigo hold on tight, or will it be making a splash of its own? Buckle up, folks, because tonight, the rodeo has gone totally ribbiting! Let's see if this dynamic duo can turn bull riding into frog flying! *Yeehaw!*"

    Lydia considered jumping into the rodeo ring to rescue Eleanor Roosevelt but then reconsidered. This was not like the pond at Graceland. There was a dangerous animal in the mix. Luckily, the rodeo clowns and bullfighters had sprung into action to calm the bull and do their job to protect the rider, even if it was a frog. But, before they could intervene, the bull unexpectedly pranced out of the ring and back to his pen.

    After the rodeo, Eleanor Roosevelt could not be found. No one knew where she went after her daring ride on a bull. Lydia looked for hours and finally, very worried, she went for help. She saw one of the medics on the scene who had witnessed Eleanor's daring ride. He was a rugged and friendly character who introduced himself as Jake.

    Jake's sun-weathered skin and a few visible scars told the story of a person who was no stranger to outdoor adventures and hands-on experiences. His eyes were keen and observant, constantly scanning his surroundings for any signs of trouble or those in need. Despite the importance of his profession, Jake had a warm and approachable demeanor, making Lydia feel at ease in his presence. She imagined his easy going nature allowed him to connect with children and adults, creating the sense of trust crucial in his line of work.

    Jake understood the urgency of finding Eleanor Roosevelt and joined Lydia in the search. They checked around the rodeo grounds, asking other event staff and attendees if they had seen a lone frog. Just when they were about to stop looking and take a break, they spotted Eleanor Roosevelt by a food stand, munching on flies that had congregated around the food. Eleanor looked embarrassed but unharmed. Lydia thanked Jake for his assistance. The medic, amused by the unique circumstances, smiled and reassured Lydia that it was all part of the unpredictable charm of the Frog Jumping festival.

"Well, that was fun," Eleanor croaked, "but it was not an experience I want to repeat. I could have gotten trampled! Thank you, Jake, for helping to find me. Don't look so surprised." She gave a deep croak. "I guess you've never heard of a talking frog before."

Jake shook his head and laughed. "I'm guessing that is something we should keep to ourselves. Good luck in the contest!"

Lydia was surprised that Eleanor Roosevelt had so quickly come to trust Jake and revealed her unusual talents, but she felt the same way.

Chapter 17
Training a frog to jump

Amos was the man in charge of the frog jumping contest and instructed the human handlers, known as 'frog jockeys,' on how to get the best performance out of their frogs. Despite his role as the head of the Calaveras County Frog Jumping Contest, there was a down-to-earth quality about him. His balding head and strands of gray hair indicated his age, while his authoritative but friendly demeanor suggested a genuine love for the event he oversaw.

"Listen, young lady," Amos told Lydia, adjusting his hat as he imparted his wisdom, "if you want that frog of yours to jump far, you better keep your hands off of it as much as possible before the contest. Frogs don't like too much fuss, you know. They need to be in their zone."

He explained the intricacies of frog behavior, even using phrases like 'let the frog be a frog' and 'they're not pets during the contest; they're athletes.' Amos lectured the contestants about the peculiarities of frog jumping and how to increase their chances of success. Despite his stern tone, there was a twinkle of amusement in Amos's eyes, recognizing the eccentric nature of the contest and the earnestness of participants like Lydia. His bossy advice was, in a way, a part of the charm and tradition of the Calaveras County Frog Jumping Contest.

Lydia nodded attentively, determined to give Eleanor Roosevelt the best chance at winning. She smiled and thanked Amos for the advice, though in her heart, she knew that Eleanor was not like the other frogs. She gently stroked Eleanor's back, sharing a reassuring look with her amphibian friend. She watched as other frog jockeys, each with their lively and energetic frogs, prepared for the qualifying events in the competition.

"Ellie, you will get three jumps. I will be in front of you singing 'Follow Me' by John Denver. If you jump the best of this year's contestants, you get a handsome brass plaque, your name in the Frog Hop Hall of Fame, and I get $5,000. But if you beat the world record set in 1986 of 21 feet, 6 inches by the frog, Rosie the Ribeter, you get a bigger plaque, a fancy trophy, and I get $20,000."

"I know, I know, I've been reading all along. No pressure here!"

"Ellie, you won't like this, but you shouldn't eat too much on the day of your big jump. Remember what happened to Dan'l Webster, the frog in Mark Twain's story. You need to be lean and mean. And your frog legs need to be warm."

So, Ellie agreed to wear a jumpsuit to keep her legs warm until the race. There were booths at the festival that sold clothing for frogs. Eleanor wasn't too keen on the idea of the jumpsuit. She was of the opinion that wearing clothing was one of the more frivolous human traditions. But Lydia thought it might help keep her legs warm. They finally settled on an aqua jumpsuit with green and pink stripes but no sequins or ruffles.

"That's where I draw the line," Ellie said firmly.

The next day, Lydia and Ellie began practicing to qualify for the big event. Though past winners of this contest had stressed the need for the jumping frog to remain as wild as possible, this was not part of their strategy. Lydia and Eleanor Roosevelt had spent too

Eleanor's Leap

much time together at this point. The bond between them was not that of owner and pet but of partners in a quest for victory. They hoped this bond would matter more than Eleanor being just another wild amphibian. They used this strategy as Eleanor made it through one qualifying event after another. And they did, indeed, make it to the final event on the final day of the jumping contest. Over 400 frogs had started, and now fifty frogs were left to compete for the actual trophies.

Chapter 18
The Frog-Jumping Contest

Lydia stood at the edge of the bustling fairgrounds, clutching the wet gunny sack that now concealed Eleanor Roosevelt. Excitement buzzed through the air. It was mid-day on the fourth and final day of the contest. The annual Calaveras County Frog-Jumping Jubilee was about to commence, and Lydia and Ellie were determined to win. Lydia hoped to win prize money, and Ellie coveted the bronze medal, acknowledging her as the best jumping bullfrog in the land. Eleanor Roosevelt croaked with excitement. She did not speak with Lydia in front of the other contestants, as that would certainly cause a major uproar.

At the start of the race, it was hard to say who was more nervous, the frogs or the jockeys. Lydia approached the registration booth, signing Eleanor up, her heart pounding with anticipation, nervousness, and excitement. The competition was fierce, with frogs of all shapes and sizes vying for the title of the longest distance in three jumps. To calm herself, Lydia put a piece of hard peppermint candy in her mouth.

The contest arena was a circular stage surrounded by cheering spectators. The atmosphere was alive with laughter, chatter, and the occasional ribbit. Lydia found a spot near the edge of the stage, Eleanor safely in her gunny sack. The announcer's voice boomed through the

Eleanor's Leap

speakers, introducing each participant and their frog with playful banter.

When it was Lydia and Eleanor's turn, Lydia removed the jumpsuit from Ellie and stepped onto the stage with Eleanor Roosevelt in her hands and a mix of pride and nerves. Amos, the announcer, amplified the excitement calling out "Eleanor Roosevelt, a contender with an inspiring famous name!"

The crowd hushed in anticipation as the countdown began. "Three, two, one, jump!" As Lydia dropped Eleanor on the starting spot, she began to sing "Follow Me," forgetting the candy in her mouth.

Eleanor Roosevelt leaped forward, her powerful hind legs propelling her through the air. The crowd erupted into cheers. As Eleanor Roosevelt soared through the air, Lydia gasped in a sudden rush of excitement, and the peppermint lodged itself in her throat. It was terrible timing.

Ellie's first jump was very high and far. Lydia clutched at her neck, eyes wide with terror as she struggled to draw breath. The crowd's cheers faded into a muffled blur as Lydia stumbled backward, desperately trying to dislodge the obstruction. Panic swept through her, threatening to overshadow the thrill of seeing Ellie jump ahead.

In the chaotic moments that followed, Lydia's vision blurred, and her strength waned. The crowd hushed, their enthusiasm turning to concern. Eleanor, having completed her triumphant first jump, croaked anxiously, seemingly aware that something was dreadfully wrong.

Turning her head Ellie saw that Lydia was kneeling on the ground, grasping at her throat. This was not how they had practiced. Lydia was supposed to be singing. What was Lydia doing? Ellie realized that Lydia needed help and fast. There was a paramedic team on the grounds, but not right there. Ellie took off, forgetting entirely about the contest. She leaped off the contest platform, out to the fairgrounds, out to where the medic truck was.

The medic, who happened to be their friend Jake, listened to Ellie with alarm. "Lydia is in grave trouble. She is thrashing about on the ground. I don't know what is wrong. She needs your help."

Jake grabbed a medic kit and ran, following the hopping frog. Ellie took off back to the frog jumping platform. Lydia was still in trouble. People were crowding around her. Jake quickly assessed the situation. With swift and practiced movements, he performed the Heimlich maneuver, dislodging the candy from Lydia's throat.

She gasped for air, relief flooding her features as color returned to her face. Initially hushed with worry, the crowd erupted into applause as Lydia took her first deep breaths. Eleanor Roosevelt stayed by her side.

Lydia sighed, "Oh, Ellie, I am so sorry. I ruined everything. All our plans. All our practicing."

Ellie consoled her, "It's okay. No problem. What would I do with a bronze metal plaque anyway? It would tarnish in the pond. But sadly, there will be no pot of money for you. I am sorry about that."

The judge, still wearing a concerned expression and trying to get Lydia's attention, approached with the trophy in hand. "We kept marking Eleanor's jumps even after she hopped off the platform. Eleanor Roosevelt jumped further than any frog has ever jumped in the entire history of the Calaveras County Frog Jumping contest!"

The judge continued, "We measured 26.8 feet in 3 jumps. It was hard to measure because this frog was so quickly out of sight. Lydia, your frog is now the all-time world champion frog jumper. She wins $20,000 in addition to the plaque. It was an amazing performance. But what is the secret of why the frog jumped to get help?"

Lydia managed a weak smile, graciously accepting the trophy. "Eleanor Roosevelt and I are a team. It may be hard to understand, but she is my very best friend. We have learned so much from each other. You'd think being so different would be a big problem, but it has offered gifts instead. You just can't imagine what you can learn from a frog!"

Eleanor Roosevelt, having once again become the center of attention, croaked triumphantly, celebrating their victory and the shared triumph over an unforeseen challenge.

Lydia beamed with pride as she and Eleanor were declared the winners of the Calaveras frog-jumping contest. The crowd erupted into applause, and Lydia couldn't contain her excitement. She hugged Eleanor tightly, overwhelmed with gratitude for her amazing lady bullfrog. But, this time, Lydia remembered not to kiss Eleanor. There were boundaries!

Amos approached Lydia and Eleanor after the crowd dispersed.

"This is a remarkable frog, you know. You could take her to many places to show off talent like that. Where do you think you'll go next?"

Lydia and Eleanor exchanged a glance, and they both knew the answer. "This has been an incredible adventure, and we have loved traveling together. But it's springtime in Alabama, and it's time for us to go home."

Epilogue
Back Home
Locust Fork, Alabama

As the sun set over the serene town of Locust Fork, Alabama, Eleanor Roosevelt and Lydia found themselves back where their extraordinary journey had begun. The quaint charm of the countryside embraced them, warmly welcoming them back from a grand adventure. It seemed like they were home in no time. They unpacked Buttercup and gave her a good wash.

The golden light of the setting sun bathed the pond behind Lydia's little home in a rosy glow. Eleanor and Lydia sat on a large, flat rock on the edge of the pond. The water shimmered with hues of orange and pink, reflecting the peaceful evening sky. Tall reeds swayed gently in the breeze, their tips brushing against the water's surface. Fireflies began to emerge, their tiny lights flickering like stars in the dusky air.

Lydia leaned back on her hands, taking a deep breath of the cool, fresh air. They sat together in silence for a while, taking in the stillness. "There is a strangeness to being back in a familiar place after a journey like that," Lydia mused. "Since everything here is pretty much the same, I can really see that I'm the one who's changed. In some ways I feel like a different person than the woman who sat here and cried into this pond.

"But, also, Ellie, I'm not really a *different* person. I'm actually more myself than I've ever been before." Lydia laughed at her own circling thoughts. She didn't know if what she was saying would make sense to most people, but she knew that Eleanor would understand.

As if she could read Lydia's mind, Eleanor croaked softly. She did understand. She had always been an extraordinary bullfrog, but she had been changed by this trip, too. She hopped closer to the water's edge, watching the widening circles ripple out from where her webbed feet touched the water. "Our journey was amazing. We saw so much, learned so much. The message from the raven was right–there really always is '*more beyond.*' Not just more places to go, but more adventures to experience, more feelings to feel, more lessons to learn, more of *life* to take in!"

Lydia's eyes gazing out over the pond. "I missed this place so much, the sound of the water, the smell of the trees, and just... the feeling of being here." They sat side by side and took in the serenity of the scene. They had witnessed some breathtaking scenery over the past weeks, but there was something different about the beauty of this place. They were not visitors here.

Lydia sighed with contentment. "I loved the excitement and lessons of that adventure. And, I also love the feeling of belonging and security that I have here in Locust Fork. I'm so grateful that we get to have both."

Eleanor nodded in agreement. "Just think–if we had never found the courage to leave, then we would never really know how good it feels to come home." They sat in companionable silence for a few moments, watching as the stars began to appear in the sky, their light twinkling in the reflection on the pond. The world around them was calm and still.

With a final, fond glance at the pond where this adventure began, Lydia rose and made her way back to

Eleanor's Leap

the warm, welcoming light of her little home. Eleanor hopped back into the serene pond, settling into her familiar resting place and joining into the familiar chorus of creatures singing their evening songs. They each were tired but happy, homesick but now home, carrying the memories and lessons of their journey.

About the Author, Sharon J. Cook

I'm a retired psychologist living in Locust Fork, Alabama, on our 14-acre plot with my husband Steve, our dog Oscar, and a three-legged cat named Leo. The Locust Fork River winds around our property. We raise most of our vegetables and have a flower garden. As in this story, the lovely setting is our place of peace and contentment. We've also explored the "beyond" traveling the world in years past. Writing this story has been pure joy for me.

About the Illustrator, Joan Babcock

Joan is a self-taught artist living and teaching in Blount County, Alabama. Each day she pushes herself to her creative limits. Sharing her art is her passion.

Acknowledgments

I am deeply grateful to Teresa (T.K.) Thorne, an award-winning fiction and nonfiction writer, who led me into this journey and remained by me, encouraging, teaching, and editing all the way through. I thank Amy Rhudy, Curator of the Blount County Memorial Museum, who believed in me and this story from the moment she first heard me talk about it and said, "I'm going to publish it!" without even reading it. I thank my husband, Steve, a first reader who helped me research what places Eleanor and Lydia should travel through on their journey to Calaveras County. Lindsey Mullen, was the assistant who helped add pizzazz to my writing and Joan Babcock brought the book to life with her beautiful illustrations. Thanks to Lynda Heines for reading my story, loving it, and taking charge of the final formatting of the book. I thank the many friends who took the time to read the story and offer helpful comments. The publisher, Joseph Lumpkin, his wife Lynn and son Breandan were very supportive and helpful in getting *Eleanor's Leap* into a real book.

Made in the USA
Columbia, SC
20 October 2024